A DARK DRABBLES ANTHOLOGY

Compiled & Edited by D Kershaw

Also available from Black Hare Press

DARK DRABBLE ANTHOLOGIES

WORLDS
ANGELS
MONSTERS
BEYOND
UNRAVEL
APOCALYPSE
LOVE
HATE
OCEANS
ANCIENTS

Twitter: @BlackHarePress
Facebook: BlackHarePress
Website: www.BlackHarePress.com

Hate, A Dark Drabbles Anthology title is
Copyright © 2020 Black Hare Press
First published in Australia in March 2020 by Black Hare Press

The authors of the individual stories retain the copyright of the works
featured in this anthology.

All characters and events in this publication, other than those clearly in the
public domain, are fictitious and any resemblance to real persons, living or
dead, is purely coincidental.

All rights reserved. No part of this production may be reproduced, stored in a
retrieval system, or transmitted, in any form or by any means, electronic,
mechanical, photocopying, recording or otherwise, without the prior
permission of the publisher and copyright owner.

Paperback : ISBN 978-1-925809-55-8
Hardcover : ISBN 978-1-925809-56-5

Cover Design by Dawn Burdett
Book Formatting by Ben Thomas

Blunted unto goodness is the heart which anger never stirreth,

But that which hatred swelleth, is keen to carve out evil.

Anger is a noble infirmity, the generous failing of the just.

The one degree that riseth above zeal, asserting the prerogatives of

virtue:

But hatred is a slow continuing crime, a fire in the bad man's breast,

A dull and hungry flame, for ever craving insatiate.

Hatred would harm another; anger would indulge itself;

Hatred is a simmering poison; anger, the opening of a valve:

Hatred destroyeth as the upas-tree; anger smiteth as a staff:

Hatred is the atmosphere of hell; but anger is known in heaven.

Is there not a righteous wrath, an anger just and holy,

When goodness is sitting in the dust, and wickedness enthroned on

Babel?

Doth pity condemn guilt? is justice not a feeling but a law

Appealing to the line and to the plummet, incognizant of moral

sense?

Thou that condemnest anger, small is thy sympathy with angels.

Thou that hast accounted it for sin, cold is thy communion with

heaven.

Martin Farquhar Tupper, *Of Hatred And Anger* **1840**

Table of Contents

Foreword.. 21

Justice by Zoey Xolton 23

Heads or Tails by G. Allen Wilbanks 24

I Caused the Holocaust by P.C. Darkcliff 25

Final Edit by J.D. Bell 26

A Controversial Opinion by Ali House.............. 27

A Scream in the Silence by J.W. Garrett........... 28

S.H.E.L.L.Y. by Brandi Hicks............................ 29

It's Heart to Hate You by Michael D. Davis...... 30

Kill Me Slowly by Umair Mirxa 31

To Sleep, Perchance to Dream by Jason Holden...... 32

Skin Peeler by Terry Miller................................ 33

Hater in a Strange Land by Carole de Monclin 34

Survivor by Terri A. Arnold 35

The Rage Book by Koji A. Dae 36

Hannah Has a Talk by Angela Zimmerman 37

Where Heartbreak Takes You by Nerisha Kemraj 38

Wishes Do Come True by Eddie D. Moore 40

Bon Appetit by K.C. Clarke 41

Sober by V. Mylynne Smith................................ 42

It Was Too Easy by Lynne Phillips..................... 43

To the Victor by Joachim Heijndermans 44

Cold by Nerisha Kemraj.................................... 45

She Swiped Right by Stephen Herczeg 46

Bonds of Holy Acrimony by Melinda Pouncey 48

Enough by Wendy Roberts 49

Curse of a Beautiful Man by Ximena Escobar.....................50

Crushed Heart by Peter J. Foote 51

Sheep and Wolf Face by C.L. Steele 52

Buddy by Eddie D. Moore 53

The Last Bus Ride by J.W. Garrett....................................54

Shucked by N.M. Brown 56

Hate Me by Cindar Harrell...57

A Lesson in Revenge by Radar DeBoard..........................58

Mince and Repeat by Shawn M. Klimek 59

Betrayal by Maxine Churchman 60

Self Loathing by N.M. Brown 61

I Hate My Boss by Gary Rubidge 62

Loving Husband, Loving Son by Galina Trefil 63

Lazy Daisy by Serena Jayne..64

Mirrors by Vonnie Winslow Crist......................................65

Loved to Bits by Andrew Anderson 66

Punching Bag Needed by Brian Rosenberger 67

The Scent of Fierce by Shawn M. Klimek.........................68

Feelings by Terri A. Arnold...69

Nosy Neighbours by Rowanne S. Carberry 70

The River Legacy by Nicola Currie 71

Excel by Lyndsey Ellis-Holloway 72

Storge by Sanziana Tamiian...74

Chow by Nicola Currie..75

The Man Within by K.B. Elijah 76

In His Hands by T.W. Garland 77

Slow Burn by Chris Bannor 78

A Hateful Spell by Shawn M. Klimek 79

Seikel's 'Hobby' by Stuart Conover 80

The Envious Mother by D.J. Elton... 82

Ruffles by Vonnie Winslow Crist 83

Meeting the Devil by Abiran Raveenthiran 84

A Man of His Word by Frances Tate.. 85

Deadly Sweetener by Peter J. Foote 86

Stung by Frances Tate.. 88

All's Fair by Carole de Monclin... 89

When the Blood Spills by Rowanne S. Carberry 90

The Argument by Chris Bannor 92

See You in Hell by Jacob Baugher... 93

In Line for a Punch by John H. Dromey.................................... 94

Drink Up by Tiegan Clyne 95

Hurts You Is Its Own Reward by John H. Dromey 96

Man of Steel by John H. Dromey... 97

Some Good Points by Paula R.C. Readman 98

The Perfect Day by Stuart Conover.. 99

You Will Remember Me by Jason Holden................................ 100

Breathing Room by Peter J. Foote 101

Wait Plan by Shawn M. Klimek 102

Dark Chocolate by Lauralana Dunne..................................... 104

Betrayed by Cassandra Angler 105

The Wedding's Off by Trisha Ridinger McKee 106

The Tyres, They Squeal by Stephen Herczeg........................ 107

A Giant's Revenge by McKenzie Richardson 108

Life After Hate by Carole de Monclin 109

Hatred for You by C.L. Williams 110

Frenemies by Wondra Vanian...................... 111

Liar by Nerisha Kemraj...................... 112

Ex Education by Raven Corinn Carluk 114

Too Late by Kelly A. Harmon 115

A Slashing Song by Shelly Jarvis...................... 116

Not the Opposite of Love by Raymond Johnson...................... 118

It's Over by Eddie D. Moore...................... 119

The Tell-Tale Art by P.C. Darkcliff...................... 120

A Strange Incident at the Cafe by Jacek Wilkos...................... 121

Would Smell as Sweet by Peter J. Foote...................... 122

Abandonment by C.L. Williams 123

Tech Era Revenge by J.M. Meyer 124

Remember Me by Terri A. Arnold...................... 125

Smiling by Owen Morgan 126

Existing by Dawn DeBraal 127

Sins of the Father by Maxine Churchman...................... 128

Modern Hate by David Bowmore...................... 129

Noise Nuisance by Jacek Wilkos...................... 130

Nightmares by K.T. Tate 131

Heartbeat by David M. Donachie...................... 132

Daydreams by G. Allen Wilbanks...................... 133

Akazawa A'avik's Revenge by Vonnie Winslow Crist.............134

Fresh Herbs by Eddie D. Moore 135

Stayin' Alive by Shelly Jarvis..................................136

The Long Con by N.M. Brown 137

Bluebeard's Bloody Test by McKenzie Richardson 138

The Hate You Make by Liam Hogan 139

Laughter by Rhiannon Bird 140

Inconvenient by Chris Bannor 141

Reflected in her Eyes by J.W. Garrett...........................142

Serial Student by Terri A. Arnold 144

Hag by Terry Miller...145

A Soldier's Revenge by Zoey Xolton 146

Ghost by Cassandra Angler.....................................147

I Am Sin by Terry Miller 148

Deconstructive Criticism by Joanna Marsh 149

One More Slash by Clint Foster.................................150

Burning Bridges by Annie Percik...............................151

Current Mood by Andrew Anderson............................152

Trail by Robin Braid 153

A Sister's Love by S.N. Graves 154

Boredom and Change by Radar DeBoard........................155

Repeat the Question by Nikki DeKeuster.........................156

Time to Put on Those Dancing Shoes by Jason Holden 157

Roasting Marshmallows by C.L. Williams 158

Silence by James Lipson 159

The Fool by Jennifer Hatfield...................................160

Road Rage by Shawn M. Klimek...................................... 161

A New Horror Story by Cindar Harrell 162

Out of Time by Dannielle Viera 163

Stupid People by Stephen Herczeg 164

A Little Bit of Torture by Jodi Jensen................................ 165

A Dance with Suspicion by Carole de Monclin 166

Jennifer's Lament by Stuart Conover 167

The Guardian by James Lipson 168

Cancer by Ximena Escobar 169

Al Moto's Revenge by J.B. Wocoski 170

Loathing by C.L. Williams.. 171

Going Down, Sir? by Andrew Anderson.......................... 172

The Last Dance by Kimberly Rei.................................... 173

My Own Vengeance by Brandi Hicks 174

Just Stop It by Stuart Conover 175

Bloody Revenge by Emma K. Leadley 176

The Case of the Tortured Torso by John H. Dromey 177

He Loves Me Not by Zoey Xolton 178

Over a Steak by C.L. Williams...................................... 179

Blackmail by Trisha Ridinger McKee 180

Waste Not, Want Not by Dale Parnell.............................. 181

The Ex by Lyndsey Ellis-Holloway 182

Bitter Tea by R.A. Goli 183

My Lover's Lover by Shelly Jarvis.................................. 184

Pre-existing Condition by Raven Corinn Carluk...................... 186

Not Enough Coffee by Zoey Xolton 187

You Said You Wouldn't, But You Did by Monica Schultz....... 188

Monster by T.W. Garland 189

New Neighbours by Kevin Berg.. 190

This Little Piggy by A.R. Dean 191

Leaving Gift by Dale Parnell... 192

Hate Runs in the Family by T.A. Ulven 193

Just a Friend by G. Allen Wilbanks.................................... 194

Meet at 0600 Hours, Top of the World Hotel by Jacob Bowers
.... 195

Prayer by Dale Parnell 196

Fury by Gabriella Balcom 197

The Best Revenge by Mikko Rauhala 198

The Illustrated Boy by Nicola Currie 199

Tea for Two by Jason Holden 200

The Press Are Vultures by Ximena Escobar 201

Last Laugh by Shelly Jarvis 202

Secret Ingredient by K.B. Elijah.. 203

Us and Them by Dawn Knox... 204

Curse by A.R. Johnston 205

Breathe by Michele Freeman 206

Home Run by Dawn DeBraal... 207

People Just Gotta Learn the Rules by Stephen Herczeg 208

Target of Hate by Tracy Davidson...................................... 210

Melanie's Choice by Lynne Phillips 211

Pincushion by Brian Rosenberger 212

Copycat by V. Mylynne Smith 213

Revenge is Sweet by Terri A. Arnold 214

The Porcupine Man by Terry Miller 215

Ashes in the Water by G. Allen Wilbanks 216

Hate Versus Love by Olivia Arieti 217

Have a Nice Fall by Clint Foster 218

Love Me Once by Umair Mirxa 219

She Even Took My Hand Cream by Stephen Herczeg 220

Janus Lot's Wife by Paula R.C. Readman 221

The Plunge by J.M. Ames 222

Hell Hath No Fury Like a Psychopath Scorned by Frances Tate
.... 223

Liar by Catherine Kenwell 224

A Growing Alarm by Maxine Churchman 226

In Time by Brianna Witte 227

A Lesson in Trust by Paula R.C. Readman 228

Smile For Me by J.W. Garrett 229

Murder She Wrote by Umair Mirxa 230

Turned Up to Eleven by Clint Foster 231

Burning in the Night by Destiny Eve Pifer 232

Infamous Last Words by John H. Dromey 233

Left at the Altar by Evelyn Benvie 234

The Last Straw by Jodi Jensen 235

The Weave by Maura Yzmore 236

Trapped by Annie Percik 237

Calista by Vonnie Winslow Crist 238

The Apartment by Trisha Ridinger McKee 239

Sweetheart by Nicola Currie 240

On Reflection by Maxine Churchman.........................241

Monsters by Chris Bannor 242

Bowline Vengeance by Michael Carter.......................243

Unconditional by A.L. King...244

Helping Hand by G. Allen Wilbanks 245

A Victim of Love by Ann Christine Tabaka 246

The Mummy of the Marsh by Matthew M. Montelione..........247

Merciless by Zoey Xolton 248

Laying the Blame by Annie Percik..............................249

A Life of Hate by Nerisha Kemraj................................250

Her Face by Dermott O'Malley 252

Sweets for My Sweetheart by Raven Corinn Carluk...............253

Home Warfare by D.J. Elton 254

Til Death Do Us Part by Nerisha Kemraj.....................256

Hate in Half the Time by Michael D. Davis 257

Heart Pain by A.S. Charly 258

Garrett by Gabriella Balcom 259

Light Bulb by Brian Rosenberger.................................260

Mean Girls by A.R. Dean 261

Guess My Name by McKenzie Richardson 262

Honour by Nicola Currie...263

The Thanksgiving Feast by Mark Kodama...................264

Stale Mate by Dawn DeBraal......................................265

Zero Hour Contracts and Bad Managers by Kevin J. Kennedy
....266

Steel Clarity by Kimberly Rei 267

Happy Anniversary by Stuart Conover 268

Lifting the Veil by Paula R.C. Readman 270

Doll Making by A.R. Johnston 271

Blood Soaked Competition by Mark Mackey 272

Plotting by A.R. Johnston 274

Money Well Spent by Eddie D. Moore 275

Yard Sale by Peter J. Foote 276

Cybele's Lament by Kate Lowe 277

Disgruntled by Raven Corinn Carluk 278

Nasty Nancy by Amber M. Simpson 279

Not Forgiven, Never Forgotten by Rich Rurshell 280

Fate of an Evil Queen by McKenzie Richardson 281

Have Some Cake by Catherine Kenwell 282

The Greatest Con Artist by Carole de Monclin 283

Worth It by Wondra Vanian 284

Circles by Steven Lord 285

Born to Kill by Brianna Witte 286

End of a Rivalry by Radar DeBoard 287

Delicacy by Cassandra Angler 288

Sauce by Kimberly Rei 289

The Last Word by Glenn R. Wilson 290

The Circle by Ximena Escobar 291

Devolution of Love by N.M. Brown 292

Venom by Joachim Heijndermans 293

The Borrower by Kathleen Halecki 294

Arachnids by Vonnie Winslow Crist 295

Ironic by Ximena Escobar...296

Cyber-Vengeance by Jo Mularczyk.................................298

Roofer by David Bowmore 299

Hunter by A.R. Dean 300

Teach Me by J.W. Garrett..301

I Hate That Rat by D.M. Burdett 302

One Night in the Lumber Camp by McKenzie Richardson 303

The Doll by Lesley Drane 304

The Last Supper by Shelly Jarvis 305

Propolis by Maura Yzmore 306

Dig Two Graves by Aaron Channel 307

Shattered Trust by Lesley Drane......................................308

In Sight by Jeff Slade..309

The Blessed Dead by Matthew M. Montelione.....................310

Patience by Stephen Christie 311

Newer Model by Dawn DeBraal 312

Karma by A.R. Johnston...313

Bloodied Lips by Hari Navarro..314

Justice for Danny by A.R. Dean.......................................315

Justified by Chris Bannor...316

Death to the Devil by A.R. Dean 317

The Plastic Anarchist by Tristan Drue Rogers 318

Marinated by Raven Corinn Carluk 319

Combustible Loathing by Terry Miller 320

Wipe Out by Dawn DeBraal...321

Witch Burning by Paula R.C. Readman 322

Baking with Magic by A.R. Johnston 323

Foreword

Hatred. All those feelings of anger, animosity and resentment that burn inside you, building up into a raging, all-encompassing fire until you can no longer control yourself.

And then, when rational thought is lost like, as Yeats described, a besom that clears the soul of everything that is not mind or sense, what depths of depravity would you sink to in order to manifest all that hate?

Freud said hate was an ego state that wishes to destroy the source of unhappiness so that to fulfil self-preservation, and boy, did these one hundred and fifty authors leave behind some destruction!

Love and kisses
D. Kershaw & Ben Thomas
Black Hare Press

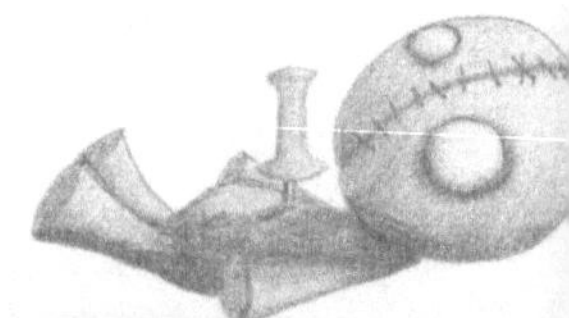

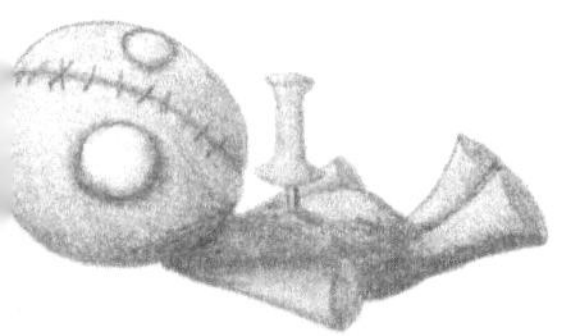

Justice
by Zoey Xolton

She throws a bucket of ice-water on the bound and gagged woman, prone on the floor. Her captive startles into consciousness, writhing pitifully, eyes wide. She smiles as the woman recognises her face, terror taking over.

"You thought you'd get away with it, didn't you?" she asks.

The woman tries to speak, but it's an exercise in futility.

"You thought there'd be no consequence? Your lies got my husband thrown in prison—an innocent man!"

Sobs. Tears.

"Your crocodile tears won't work on me, sweetheart," she says, brandishing a blowtorch. "You had your fun, now it's *my* turn to play."

Zoey Xolton is an Australian Speculative Fiction writer, primarily of Dark Fantasy, Paranormal Romance and Horror. She is also a proud mother of two and is married to her soul mate. Outside of her family, writing is her greatest passion. She is especially fond of short fiction and is working on releasing her own themed collections in future.
Website: www.zoeyxolton.com

Heads or Tails
by G. Allen Wilbanks

"They say love and hate are just two sides of the same coin," said Brent. He reached into his pocket and removed a quarter. He held it up so his wife could see it. "Heads, I used to love you so much I married you. Tails, I can't stand the sight of you now."

"The feeling is mutual," his wife assured him, throwing clothing into a suitcase.

Brent flipped the quarter and snatched it out of the air with one hand.

"What are you doing?" his wife asked.

"Heads, I let you go. Tails, you never leave this room alive."

G. Allen Wilbanks is a member of the Horror Writers Association (HWA) and has published over 100 short stories in various magazines and on-line venues. He is the author of two short story collections, and the novel, When Darkness Comes. Website: www.gallenwilbanks.com Blog: DeepDarkThoughts.com

I Caused the Holocaust
by P.C. Darkcliff

When I dropped my pants, Eva gasped into the silence of her bedroom.

"Not bad, huh?" I grinned.

"Average!" she barked. "But—you're circumcised! Adolf would kill me if he found out."

"You said he doesn't mind your affairs."

"That's true, when I cheat on him with Aryans!"

The door flew open, and Adolf strutted in. We all froze. His eyes filled with wrath at the sight of my circumcision. Although he wanted to attack me, he stomped out: the world's biggest bully was cowardly without his thugs.

Adolf got his revenge years later, though…on me and my people.

P.C. Darkcliff is the author of two novels, Deception of the Damned and The Priest of Orpagus. In September 2020, he's going to launch Celts and the Mad Goddess, the first installment of The Deathless Chronicle.
Social Media: plu.us/p.c.darkcliff
Reader List: mailchi.mp/c5550d315607/pcdarkcliff

Final Edit
by J.D. Bell

Too many adjectives. Weak characters. Poor dialogue. On…and on…and on. There is no satisfying her. She has no appreciation for the time and effort I put into my story. None whatsoever.

I wonder how she liked my latest work? The tale of the editor who has no heart. The editor who destroyed the dreams of a passionate writer. The editor who cried like a whimpering child when she learned of her fate. I will never know. The knife penetrated deep and blood is pouring from her gaping wound. Is this what she meant by show, do not tell?

J.D. Bell is an award-winning, internationally published, author of flash fiction and short stories. He recently retired from the world of writing advertising copy and is now enjoying the universe of creative fiction.
Facebook: jim.writes.stories
Twitter: @JimBell58

A Controversial Opinion
by Ali House

The glowing flames illuminated his face as he stared at the burning fields, the warm Brazilian night made warmer by the blaze. Although he delighted in the sight, he wouldn't allow himself to smile. He'd travelled so far, and yet he wasn't done. There were more fields to burn.

One day he would be rid of them, and on that day he would rest. On that day he'd smile wide and happy, knowing that all of the pineapple farms had been destroyed. He'd show the world—he'd show everyone—and there would be no more pineapple on pizza ever again.

Ali House is the author of sci-fi/fantasy novels The Six Elemental and The Fifth Queen, along with various short stories in the "From the Rock" series published by Engen Books. She is a traveller, baker, and fan of the Oxford comma. Website: engenbooks.com/tag/house-blog/

A Scream in the Silence
by J.W. Garrett

Scott heard footfalls. Then not. After a divergence in the path, Brian no longer followed. The trap had worked. He'd headed deeper into the mine's depths. Now Scott might not even be able to find him. The bowels of the mine were maze like. Scott knew them well but didn't venture into the centre without a buddy.

A scream echoed.

About now Brian would be surrounded by pitch black, scared, hope fading, disoriented, despair sinking deep into his gut. Scott understood from Brian's daily torment…laughing at him, watching him bleed.

Emerging alone, Scott heaved a breath and headed home.

J.W. Garrett has been writing in one form or another since she was a teenager. She currently lives in Florida with her family but loves the mountains of Virginia where she was born. Her writings include YA fantasy as well as short stories. Since completing Remeon's Quest-Earth Year 1930, the prequel in her YA fantasy series, Realms of Chaos, she has been hard at work on the next in the series, scheduled to release August 2020. When she's not hanging out with her characters, her favourite activities are reading, running and spending time with family.
Website: www.jwgarrett.com
BHC Press: www.bhcpress.com/Author_JW_Garrett.html

S.H.E.L.L.Y.
by Brandi Hicks

My boss—my ex-boss—lay naked and spread-eagled on the table, mumbling something. I didn't care what he was trying to say, that's why I had him gagged and his arms and legs strapped tightly to the table. I leaned over so I was face to face with him.

"You thought you could just grab my ass and make passes at me, then have the nerve to fire me? No way, you vile excuse for a man. You'll never harass another woman again."

I grabbed his shrivelled dick, brought my scalpel up to it, and began carving my name: S…

*Growing up in West Virginia, **Brandi Hicks** loved to have her nose in a book, her eyes toward the night sky and putting a pen to paper. Her imagination was always sparked by her grandfather and her mom taking her to new places and teaching her about the unusual. She loves fantasy, sci-fi, and learning about science and history. She has two beautiful children, and hopes to instill creativity and a love of reading in them. Finding new crafts to try keeps her busy when not playing with her kids or working.*

It's Heart to Hate You
by Michael D. Davis

I have the heart of a small child, the heart of a middle-aged woman, and the heart of an elderly man all on my bookshelf. The kid spat at me, the woman cut me off in traffic, and the old bastard was just being an old bastard. It doesn't take much to hate a person, it takes even less to kill one.

The newest heart is on my nightstand right beside my bed. At night with the moon coming in through the window, the heart looks so beautiful. This is the only way my wretched husband will ever be beautiful.

Michael D. Davis was born and raised in a small town in the heart of Iowa. Having written over thirty short stories, ranging in genre from comedy to horror from flash fiction to novella he continues in his accursed pursuit of a career in the written word.

Kill Me Slowly
by Umair Mirxa

Katrina stood in the shadows, observing from behind a tree. Here, at long last, her decade-long search was at an end.

She waited until he turned away. The throw was practised, her aim perfect. He staggered and fell to his knees.

"You took from me," she said, looking down at him in contempt. "All I ever loved."

"Ah. So, you have come for revenge. Have at it, darling. Kill me slowly."

He smiled up at her look of surprise, but it lasted only a moment. Katrina took a second stake from her belt and plunged it deep into his heart.

Umair Mirxa lives and writes in Karachi, Pakistan. His first published story, 'Awareness', appeared on Spillwords Press. He has since had stories accepted for publication in anthologies from Zombie Pirate Publishing, Blood Song Books, Black Hare Press, Iron Faerie Publishing, Clarendon House Publications, Fantasia Divinity Magazine & Publishing, and The ReAnimated Writers Press. He is a massive J.R.R. Tolkien fan, loves everything to do with mythology, fantasy, and history, and wishes with all his heart that dragons were real. When he's not writing, he enjoys reading novels and comic books, playing video games, listening to music, and watching movies, TV shows, and football as an Arsenal FC fan.
Website: umairmirxa.com

To Sleep, Perchance to Dream
by Jason Holden

It's hard enough to sleep after a night shift, without that idiot revving his car, blasting his "Gangster" rap while showing off to his mates.

Today was the last straw. We'd had the usual morning ritual, me trying to sleep. Him noisily revving his engine before setting off for a joy ride.

His dog kept barking. I went, shouted at it. It barked more.

I kicked it. Kicked it. Kicked it until nothing was left but bloody pulp.

I dragged it to the front and smeared "SHUT UP!" in bloody letters across his drive. Maybe now he'll get the message.

Jason Holden is a human. He lives here and there in the UK, always with his wife, daughter and fur baby. His primary goal is to raise his daughter to adulthood without any major damage. When he can, he writes. He thinks he does it well, but you can be the judge of that. He has been published in a few anthologies here and there, has been praised and put down for his writing. You can find and follow him on Facebook, although he asks you only follow him on Facebook and not through the streets. That's just creepy.
Facebook: Jason Holden-Author

Skin Peeler
by Terry Miller

Hugh was sick of trying to prove himself. He figured he might as well be the monster Chloe feared him to be since he'd never be free of her suspicions. Truth was, HUGH WAS SICK. A lifetime of rejections and heartbreaks gave him quite the distaste for the female gender as a whole.

The potato peeler sliced strips of Chloe's flesh as she screamed into the shirt stuffed in her mouth. Hugh wasn't heartless though—he did cleanse her wounds with alcohol. *Wouldn't want them to get infected, right?* After all, he was just beginning to enjoy the muted cries.

Terry Miller lives in Portsmouth, Ohio. His work has been featured in Sanitarium Magazine, Devolution Z, Jitter, Rhysling Anthology 2017, Poetry Quarterly, Sirens Call Ezine, The Horror Tree's Trembling With Fear, SpillWords, Organic Ink Vol. I, Curses & Cauldrons Anthology from Blood Song Books, Forest of Fear from Blood Song Books, the Dark Drabble Anthology Series from Black Hare Press, 100 Word Zombie Bites from Reanimated Writers Press, Scary Snippets, Guilty Pleasures & Other Dark Delights, 100 Word Horrors 3, and O Unholy Night In Deathlehem from Grinning Skull Press. Facebook: tmiller2015
Amazon: amazon.com/author/millerterry1

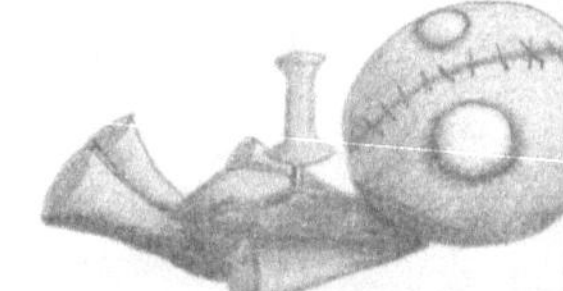

Hater in a Strange Land
by Carole de Monclin

Leaving it anywhere will provide the same outcome.

But I give it, masquerading as a flower, to a little girl in a park.

Destruction starting with one innocent. Intoxicating idea.

No.

No human deserves to be called innocent. They all carry the seeds of viciousness.

I witnessed their cruelty.

The girl smiles her thank you, but trivial emotions won't touch me.

I crossed the void with a single purpose.

She'll die first, then, like an unstoppable tide, the microbe will swallow loathsome humankind.

Bloodlust satisfied, I cry for my mate, killed by a human explorer.

My hatred spent, hollowness remains.

Carole de Monclin travels both the real world and imaginary ones. She's lived in France, Australia, and the USA; visited 25+ countries; and explored Mars, Ceres, and many distant planets. She writes to invite people on a journey. Her stories can be found in The Arcanist, The Deep Space Anthology, and every volume of the Dark Drabbles series.
Website: *CaroledeMonclin.com*
Twitter: *@CaroledeMonclin*

Survivor
by Terri A. Arnold

I rub a hand tentatively over my bruised face, I can hardly believe I actually had the courage to free myself from this hell. I cringe as the salty tears sting as they roll down over my split lip.

I have never felt so much relief as I gaze at his lifeless body, blood slowly pooling around his head. I've hated him for four long years, but he will never hurt anyone again.

I step around him, exiting through the back door, just as the police enter through the front. Tucking my head down, I disappear into the dark night.

Terri A. Arnold is an avid reader turned writer from a small town in Nova Scotia, who has spent her life reading and wishing she was writing. Although she has written a lot in those years, she has only recently begun to submit pieces for publication. With ongoing encouragement from family and writing challenges with friends, Arnold felt the urge to try her hand at publishing.

The Rage Book
by Koji A. Dae

The cover was nondescript, the blank pages sturdy. With a glass pen dunked in blood red ink, Amber slashed her rage across the page. In swift strokes she told the book how Diane stole her boyfriend and Tiffany mocked her.

She didn't know the angry words would steal Diane's breath until she turned blue or clamp Tiffany's teeth around her tongue so forcefully she would never speak again. Of course, if they hadn't filched her hate book, they'd had been fine. Amber slipped the book in her backpack and thought about how to describe the pain her ex had caused.

Koji A. Dae is an American writer living in Bulgaria. She has work published with Tales from the Moonlit Path and ParABnormal Magazine, and forthcoming with Daily Science Fiction. When not writing, she can be found dancing the blues. Website: kojiadae.ink

Hannah Has a Talk
by Angela Zimmerman

"Well, thank God that's over," Hannah said into the hole she was quickly trying to empty. "I didn't think it was ever going to end." The service had been long. Hannah hated every minute of it.

"I promised Clark your leftover pills if he would skip out tonight. So now we don't have to worry. We can finally have that talk, Mom."

When the shovel struck the casket lid, Hannah smiled. Sweat poured down her face as she used her bloody hands to break open the seal on the casket.

"You're gonna listen now, bitch. You don't have a choice."

Angela Zimmerman is a writer living in the Southern United States. She has been published in Unnerving Magazine and Coffin Bell. You can find her personal writings at Conjure and Coffee.
Website: conjureandcoffee.com

Where Heartbreak Takes You
by Nerisha Kemraj

Can you hear the thunder roar?

As her heart screams out in pain

Can you see the oceans rise?

As her tears fall in vain

Can you see the mountains crumble?

As her resolve turns into dust?

Can you see the flashing sky?

Jolts of betrayal and mistrust

Can you feel the earth vibrate?

As her body shakes with rage

Can you see the wreck you made?

Her body fills with hate,

her entire being aches

Can you hear the deafening silence?

Her mind begs to numb emotion

Can you see the day turn to nightfall?

Each breath—an aberration

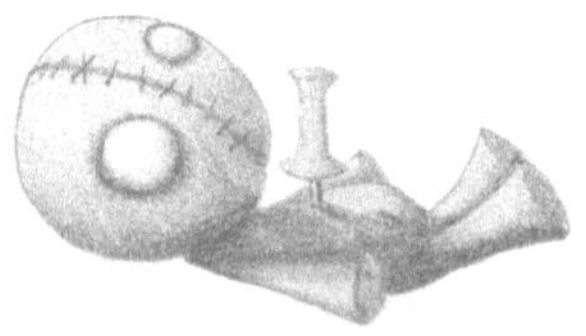

Nerisha Kemraj *resides in Durban, South Africa with her husband and two mischievous daughters. Writing since 2017, she has had over 100 short stories and poems published in various publications, both print and online. She has also received an Honourable Mention Award for her tanka in the Fujisan Taisho 2019 Tanka Contest. She holds a Bachelor's degree in Communication Science, and a Post Graduate Certificate in Education from University of South Africa.*
Amazon: amazon.com/author/nerisha_kemraj
Facebook: Nerishakemrajwriter

Wishes Do Come True
by Eddie D. Moore

Julia handed the bartender forty-five dollars to settle her bill and turned to leave, but Sandy stopped her before she reached the door.

"Hey, you promised me that you'd do a birthday shot with me." Sandy motioned to the shot-glasses on the table. As Julia turned up the glass, Sandy said, "Make a wish."

Julia slammed the glass down and said sarcastically, "I wish my ex-husband all the happiness in the world." She was still laughing when she reached her car.

Dan dialled 911 when his ex-wife drove off but dropped his phone when she was hit by the train.

Eddie D. Moore travels hundreds of hours a year, and he fills that time by listening to audiobooks. When he isn't playing with his grandchildren, he writes his own stories. You can find a list of his publications on his blog or by visiting his Amazon Author Page. While you're there, be sure to pick up a copy of his mini-anthology Misfits & Oddies.
Website: eddiedmoore.wordpress.com
Amazon: amazon.com/author/eddiedmoore

Bon Appetit
by K.C. Clarke

Trudy placed a slice of pot roast onto Tom's plate next to his mashed potatoes.

Tom happily took a bite. Then another.

"You only make your roast on special occasions."

A beaming smile arced across Trudy's face.

Without warning, a searing pain stopped Tom from taking another bite. He clutched his stomach and struggled to breathe. The room spun, and he reached out to Trudy. She just sat there, legs crossed, sipping her Champagne.

"Help me!" Tom pleaded.

"You promised you'd never cheat again," said Trudy.

Tom slumped from his chair, falling to the floor.

"You should've kept your promise."

K.C. Clarke is a new author working on her debut novel, Little Black Dress, due out early 2020. She's been published in a handful of anthologies under various pen names. When she isn't writing, she spends her days with her husband and two girls in Toronto, watching movies and playing the piano. She's also a fur mama to two rescue dogs. She loves to write romance, but her true love is fantasy, stemming from her love of JRR Tolkien and Neil Gaiman. She's a self-diagnosed caffeine and pickle addict, an ailment for which she does not wish to seek treatment.

Sober
by V. Mylynne Smith

The constant arguing is enough to drive any sober person sane. I've only been sober for six months, as she frequently reminds me. She's a hypocrite that guzzles wine like a fiend.

My mother sits on her high horse drinking a delicious red that I've paired with cyanide. This is her routine every night while I sit on the couch salivating, lusting after the drink in her hand, even though I know it's poison.

She's getting weaker and starting to slow down. Soon she'll have no breath to criticise. She'll be gone, and I'll be able to have a drink.

V. Mylynne Smith primarily writes thrillers, but sometimes dips a toe into horror. Her love of psychology helps her craft malicious characters with the worst intentions. She aims to create twists and turns that keep the reader guessing until the end. Smith is an Oklahoman that moved to Northwest Arkansas after meeting her husband. The pair live together in a cozy house with two pets: a pitbull named Renegade and a feisty cat named Bandit. When Smith isn't stringing words together, you can find her in front of a mirror with make-up in hand or baking something delicious and fattening.

It Was Too Easy
by Lynne Phillips

She loved him; how could he betray her?

It was the little things, perfume in his hair, new underwear, a smudge of lipstick, the diamond necklace hidden in his drawer and the furtive phone calls.

Her love slowly turned to hate, and she plotted her revenge.

It was too easy. Their assets were in her name, in case his business folded.

She sold everything, established an account with a Swiss bank, and booked into a clinic for a complete overhaul.

"See you when you get back," he said, relieved to be see her go.

She didn't plan to come back.

Lynne Phillips, a retired teacher, lives in the beautiful Northern Rivers Region of New South Wales Australia. Her stories, across all genres, have been published in anthologies and various online magazines. Her priority is spending time with her family. Her passions are reading, writing and keeping fit.

To the Victor
by Joachim Heijndermans

I won. *You* said that I could never triumph over the powers of justice and good. But *I* won. *I* was the one who jammed the power spear through your heart. *I* am the one who sits on your father's throne. *I* rule it all and you're dead, so fuck you!

Yes, the others left. They all rolled aside the moment there was nothing left to gain. They got what they wanted, so why stick around? Why do I? Why is the hate still so strong. I won. I beat you? But why can't I stop hating you?

Stupid skull.

Joachim Heijndermans writes, draws, and paints nearly every waking hour. Originally from the Netherlands, he's been all over the world, boring people by spouting random trivia. His work has been featured in a number of anthologies and publications, such as Mad Scientist Journal, Asymmetry Fiction, Hinnom Magazine, Ahoy Comics's Edgar Allan Poe's Snifter of Terror, Metaphorosis and The Gallery of Curiosities, and he's currently in the midst of completing his first children's book.
Website: www.joachimheijndermans.com
Twitter: @jheijndermans

Cold
by Nerisha Kemraj

Johnny glowered. How dare she flirt with others? He hated that she never looked at him that way. Hatred coursed through his veins.

"Johnny, would you mind covering for me for a short while?" she asked, without looking away from her new plaything.

His fists clenched.

"No problem," he said.

But he didn't stay behind the bar. Instead, he followed them towards the stock room, bolting the door behind them. He turned the air-con to full blast.

Thankfully, no one would be down for a few hours.

Yes, she deserved to feel a fraction of the cold he felt inside.

Nerisha Kemraj resides in Durban, South Africa with her husband and two mischievous daughters. Writing since 2017, she has had over 100 short stories and poems published in various publications, both print and online. She has also received an Honourable Mention Award for her tanka in the Fujisan Taisho 2019 Tanka Contest. She holds a Bachelor's degree in Communication Science, and a Post Graduate Certificate in Education from University of South Africa.
Amazon: *amazon.com/author/nerisha_kemraj*
Facebook: *Nerishakemrajwriter*

She Swiped Right
by Stephen Herczeg

She looked down at her phone. Another cavalcade of potentials showed up on her feed. Pathetic losers every one of them. She detested the thought of even communicating with them, let alone inviting them out on dates.

But, she had a job to do.

The head priest needed fresh blood for the sacrifices.

And she wanted to rise through the ranks from potentate to priestess.

That was her task. Seek them out. Make contact. Lure them in. Drug and secure them to the altar. Simple.

Ping.

A likely target appeared. She read his bio. Total loser. Perfect.

She swiped right.

Stephen Herczeg *is an IT Geek based in Canberra Australia. He has been writing for over twenty years and has completed a couple of dodgy novels, sixteen feature length screenplays and numerous short stories and scripts. His horror work has featured in Sproutlings, Hells Bells, Below the Stairs, Trickster's Treats #1 and #2, Shades of Santa, Behind the Mask, Beyond the Infinite; The Body Horror Book, Anemone Enemy, Petrified Punks and Beginnings. He has also had numerous Sherlock Holmes stories published through the Belanger Books - Sherlock Holmes anthologies.*

Amazon: amazon.com/-/e/B07916SQQS

Facebook: stephenherczegauthor

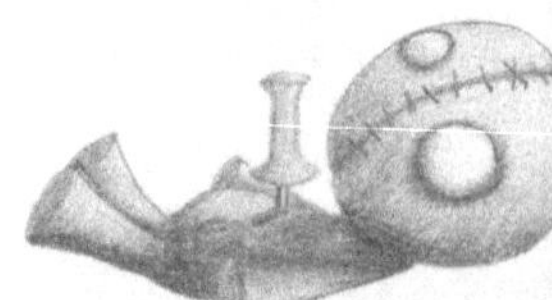

Bonds of Holy Acrimony
by Melinda Pouncey

The sight of him makes me sick!

We were happy in the beginning, but couples usually are, aren't they? Then things began to change. Cold silences became arguments, arguments sparked anger, anger exploded into violence.

My friends said I should stand up to him. My family told me to leave. Yet where could I go? They offered me no help, no real solutions. Eventually they grew tired of my waffling, leaving me mired in fear and increasing isolation.

Despite everything, or rather because of it, I can never leave him now.

If I do, the police will discover the body.

Melinda Pouncey *is a retired psychologist who enjoys exploring the complexities and scope of the human imagination through a variety of genres. From an early age, Melinda discovered an affinity for tales involving the unusual and the macabre, especially those with a dash of humour or the unexpected. She has written numerous short stories and poems, focusing her attention most recently on the horror and fantasy realms. Melinda is a member of two local writing groups and enjoys acting as an editor and proofreader when not working on stories of her own.*

Enough
by Wendy Roberts

It started out small. Little notes to remind of him what he'd done that was so very wrong because Andrew didn't know how else to make him pay. Police said there wasn't enough evidence to convict him for the hit and run, which was bullshit; he watched the cameras himself. They just didn't want to convict the man that lined their pockets. But soon the letters weren't satisfying enough, and as Andrew crushed the dog's head to even things out between them, he knew one day, not even this was going to be enough to exact revenge for his daughter.

Writing short stories and novels started as a past time for **Wendy Roberts** *and has now become a fully fledged passion. She posts short stories on her website and can be found most days on Twitter.*
Website: flippinscribbler.com
Twitter: @_WARoberts

Curse of a Beautiful Man
by Ximena Escobar

The beautiful man would live, as long as he didn't get to know himself.

Unable to wash away the guilt of breaking yet another man's heart, he stepped out of the running bath. His fogged reflection appeared in the mirror, but nothing could blur his sight of the ugly truth.

The water level rising, cracks spread like a swastika under his fist.

He still looked pretty, lying there on the tiles; glass embedded like jewels in his wrist, pouring into the flood the crimson watercolour of his soul.

As life faded dreadfully to black, he could only hate himself more.

Ximena Escobar is writing stories and poetry. Originally from Chile, she is the author of a translation into Spanish of the Broadway Musical "The Wizard of Oz", and of an original adaptation of the same, "Navidad en Oz", both produced in her home country. Since 2018 she has published several short stories in various anthologies and online platforms, and is now slowly working on her own collection. Ximena has a degree in Arts & Communication Science and lives in Nottingham with her family.
Facebook: *Ximenautora*
Twitter: *@laximenin*

Crushed Heart
by Peter J. Foote

"Madam, I can't crush this car, it's worth a fortune."

"Listen, I showed you the ownership papers, it's mine to do with as I wish, now crush it."

"Whatever lady, you're crazy." Hydraulics pistons active, metal groans.

"That's want my husband thought as well before he died. Didn't realise I found out he was hiding money from the tax man by putting everything in my name."

The roof buckles, glass shatters, a classic car is destroyed.

"When did your husband die?"

Pistons retract, the car is now nothing but scrap.

"Hmmm? Oh, he died about ten seconds ago, I'd say."

Peter J. Foote is a bestselling speculative fiction writer from Nova Scotia. Outside of writing, he runs a used bookstore specialising in fantasy & sci-fi, cosplays, and alternates between red wine and coffee as the mood demands. His short stories can be found in both print and in ebook form, with his story "Sea Monkeys" winning the inaugural "Engen Books/Kit Sora, Flash Fiction/Flash Photography" contest in March of 2018. As the founder of the group "Genre Writers of Atlantic Canada", Peter believes that the writing community is stronger when it works together.
Twitter: @PeterJFoote1
Website: peterjfooteauthor.wordpress.com

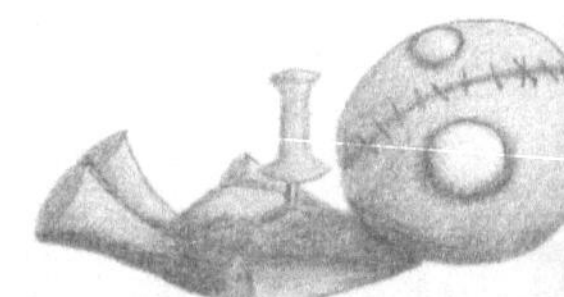

Sheep and Wolf Face
by C.L. Steele

"Two-faced idiot," she sighed as her teacher discussed Salinger's *Catcher in The Rye*. Keep your childhood innocence, protect women, youth is better; the sheep side of his two-face lecture. Banning books for language seemed antithetical to learning transition. Child one day, adult the next? Nothing in nature works like that. I believed sheep talk. Until, I heard you judge the cheerleader and the twirler, not for skill, but their uniforms. Which, by the way, they're required to wear. Pretending innocence, we hide adult vices. Does adulthood mean being two-faced? No wonder we rebel. "Idiocy," she screamed, catching society's given baton.

C.L. Steele creates new worlds and mystical places filled with complex characters on exciting journeys. Her typical genre is Sci-Fi/Fantasy, where she concentrates on writing in the sub-genres of Magical Realism, Near Future, and Futuristic worlds. Published in numerous anthologies, she looks forward to the release of her debut novel. In the interim, she works on other novels and continues to write short stories, novellas, and poetry. She is featured as one of five international authors in ICWG Magazine through Clarendon Publishing House and is a contributing author to Blood Puddles Literary Journal. Facebook: author.CLSteele Instagram: @clsteele.author

Buddy
by Eddie D. Moore

Charles heard his ex-wife calling for her dog across the street. He saw on her face how much she hated the idea of him moving into their rental house and living so close together when his attorney suggested the idea. Her expression still brought a smile to his face.

The shouts for Buddy slowed, and Charles peeked through the blinds until his ex-wife went back inside. When the front door closed, Charles sighed and walked into the kitchen. He lifted the crockpot's lid and poked at the meat.

"Some say revenge is best served cold. I don't think so, Buddy."

Eddie D. Moore travels hundreds of hours a year, and he fills that time by listening to audiobooks. When he isn't playing with his grandchildren, he writes his own stories. You can find a list of his publications on his blog or by visiting his Amazon Author Page. While you're there, be sure to pick up a copy of his mini-anthology Misfits & Oddities.
Website: eddiedmoore.wordpress.com
Amazon: amazon.com/author/eddiedmoore

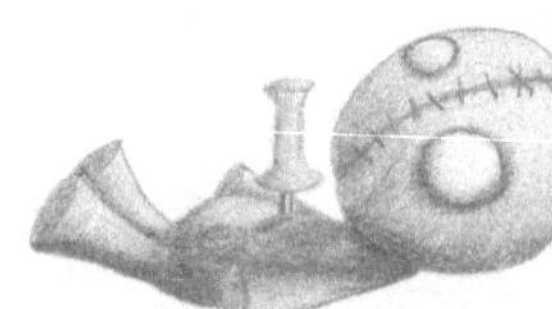

The Last Bus Ride
by J.W. Garrett

The taunting, slurs, the muttered words of loathing—day after day…

No more.

She dodged his attempt to trip her, catching his insult.

"Ugly."

Sliding into an empty bus seat, she faced the gloom outside.

She heard approaching steps, smelled his presence as he squished beside her, slamming her against the cool window.

No one helped. They never did. The driver turned a blind eye.

Wheeling on him, she entered his mind, cutting through his thoughts with the power she'd refined.

Face frozen, he slumped.

The bus lurched. Sidestepping his twitching form, she exited, a smirk falling across her face.

J.W. Garrett *has been writing in one form or another since she was a teenager. She currently lives in Florida with her family but loves the mountains of Virginia where she was born. Her writings include YA fantasy as well as short stories. Since completing Remeon's Quest-Earth Year 1930, the prequel in her YA fantasy series, Realms of Chaos, she has been hard at work on the next in the series, scheduled to release August 2020. When she's not hanging out with her characters, her favourite activities are reading, running and spending time with family.*

Website: www.jwgarrett.com
BHC Press: www.bhcpress.com/Author_JW_Garrett.html

Shucked
by N.M. Brown

My former partner had stolen my business, my financial stability, and my personal integrity. There was only one place I could go to find him; to make him pay for ruining my life.

Madame Joilee lived far out in the cornfields. You couldn't find her unless you really wanted to; she designed it that way.

She never told me his location, only offered me a stalk of corn instead. She told me that as the stalk decayed, so would he.

The day after the last husk fell, police found his body with the skin sloughed off.

I celebrated with wine.

*Since **N.M. Brown** made her first post to a popular Internet forum, she's taken the horror community by storm. Her ability to create, terrify, and drive home her stories is insurmountable. N.M. Brown's published works can be found in multiple anthologies for all to read, but be forewarned, if you do... you may want to call your therapist after, her stories are terrifying, disturbing and devilishly unsettling. She is not only a fright visually, but also has a creepy tentacle in horror podcasting as well. Sinister Sweetheart writes, voice acts and is the media director of the Scarecrow Tales podcast.*
Website: Sinistersweetheart.wixsite.com/sinistersweetheart
Facebook: NMBrownStories

Hate Me
by Cindar Harrell

You said you loved me once. You claimed that I was the only one for you. Now? I am nothing.

I watch you through the windows. I don't want you back. No, that ship has sailed.

But I can't forgive you.

I sigh as I pour the can of gasoline around your house. You're asleep, the ghost of a family dinner left on the table. A dinner without me.

That's alright. I have a new love too: fire. I throw the match onto the gasoline, and for a moment, I think I see you watching me.

Go ahead, hate me.

Cindar Harrell loves fairy tales, especially ones with a dark twist. Her writing is often fairy tale inspired, but she also loves mystery and horror. Her stories can be found in various anthologies from publishers such as Black Hare Press, Iron Faerie Publishing, Dragon Soul Press, Blood Song Books, Soteira Press, Fantasia Divinity and more. Traveling is a passion for her as it inspires her imagination to run wild, especially in places that have a mystic presence in the air. She regularly moonlights as another human, but no matter who she is, she is always writing. Her novella inspired by The Snow Queen is set to release in 2020 as well as her debut novel, Lithium, and short story collection, Perchance to Dream. Facebook: CindarHarrell

A Lesson in Revenge
by Radar DeBoard

Leopold truly hated his schoolmaster. He hated his teaching and his mannerisms when he talked. Most of all, Leopold hated how the schoolmaster tried to humiliate him at every possible opportunity. Leopold wanted nothing more than to take his revenge.

Yet he had been taught long ago, that simply killing a man is not in itself revenge. A transgressor must be made to suffer. You must take everything from them and drive them to the brink. Then you teach them of pain. So, when the schoolmaster came home to the disembowelled remains of his family, it was only the beginning.

Radar DeBoard *is a horror movie and novel enthusiast who resides in the small town of Goddard, Kansas. He occasionally dabbles in writing, and enjoys to make dark tales for people to enjoy. He has had drabbles and short stories published in various electronic magazines and anthologies.*
Facebook: WriterRadarDeBoard

Mince and Repeat
by Shawn M. Klimek

Jacqueline had worn a wide-brimmed hat over a blonde wig to evade the security cameras in her ex's apartment complex. Riding the elevator, contemplating the awful revenge in her purse, she had hesitated. Was it too late to back out? Hatred said, "Yes." If someone confronted her, she decided, she could simply hand over the spare key, pretending this had been her purpose.

The break-in went smoothly, and she was still holding the bedspread when a low growl alerted her to his girlfriend's pit bull. In a panic, Jacqueline had jumped under the sheets, inconveniently forgetting about the powdered glass.

Shawn M. Klimek is the middle child of seven creative siblings, a globetrotting, U.S. military spouse, an internationally best-selling short-story writer, award-winning poet, and butler to a Maltese. More than one hundred and fifty of his stories and poems have been published in digital magazines or anthologies, including BHP's Deep Space, Eerie Christmas and every book so far in the Dark Drabbles series.
Website: jotinthedark.blogspot.com
Facebook: shawnmklimekauthor

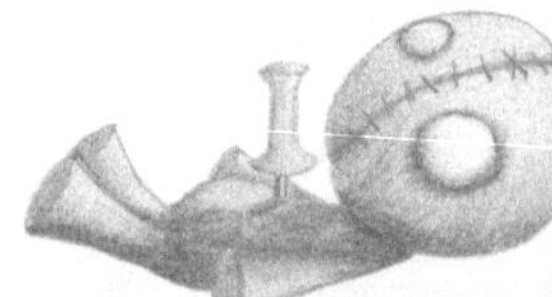

Betrayal
by Maxine Churchman

I loved him, and his betrayal cut me deeply. I drag the knife slowly across his flesh so he knows how it feels. His muffled screams soothe the hurt he caused me.

Unable to move, he glances sideways at her body, broken and discarded on the floor.

The two of them broke my heart. Does he know how that feels? Raising both fists high above my head, I bring the handle of the knife down into the centre of his chest. I understand a blow like that could kill someone, but to be sure, I smother him with a pillow.

Maxine Churchman lives in Essex UK and has recently started writing poetry and short stories to share. Her interests include learning to improve her writing, reading, knitting, walking and teaching yoga. She is also planning a novel.

Self Loathing
by N.M. Brown

The choices I've made make me want to shed my skin in shame. Even worse is, I'd likely do them again.

My mirror shows hollow pits hiding inside smiling eyes. Hairline cracks in the glass multiply the image of what I've become.

I drown my self loathing with indulgence. Cigarette packs by the day, alcohol and drugs feel so nice. Bringing me aids for my own destruction feel so nice.

People say to accept yourself. They don't crave the things I do. Pierced hearts, final breaths, pleading eyes before light leaves them.

The only hatred I know is towards myself.

*Since **N.M. Brown** made her first post to a popular Internet forum, she's taken the horror community by storm. Her ability to create, terrify, and drive home her stories is insurmountable. N.M. Brown's published works can be found in multiple anthologies for all to read, but be forewarned, if you do... you may want to call your therapist after, her stories are terrifying, disturbing and devilishly unsettling. She is not only a fright visually, but also has a creepy tentacle in horror podcasting as well. Sinister Sweetheart writes, voice acts and is the media director of the Scarecrow Tales podcast.*
Website: Sinistersweetheart.wixsite.com/sinistersweetheart
Facebook: NMBrownStories

I Hate My Boss
by Gary Rubidge

The gun pointed at me betrays the calmness on his face.

I sneer at the fool. "What do you want from me? I don't have time for this."

"Revenge," he says, matter of factly. "You sacked me last year for no reason. Now I'm gonna sack you."

"What? You're mental!" I croak, trying to place his face.

"I'm gonna shoot you, cut you up and place you in this sack here," he states triumphantly, lifting the sack in his other hand.

My God, he's serious!

My brain screams out as he laughs maniacally, but the trigger has already been pulled.

Gary Rubidge currently resides in Western Australia and is a newcomer to writing, having reached the age of 50 without consideration to authoring anything other than work reports. Encouraged by friends to put his ideas to paper he has finally taken the plunge and this is his first effort. There are many more ideas begging to be released and they are lining up to be put to paper.

Loving Husband, Loving Son
by Galina Trefil

At his trial, the serial killer said that his wife had known; that the blood-soaked signs had been so obvious that it would have been impossible for her not to avoid the grizzly knowledge.

Was his desire to have her unfairly condemned as an accessory because he refused to let her find happiness again once he was gone?

No. He'd virtually married his mother. He could admit that now. And whose abuse had warped him into being a monster in the first place?

He'd see to it that Mommy would be his final victim. Even if it wasn't really her.

Galina Trefil is a novelist specializing in women's, minority, and disabled rights. Her favorite genres are horror, thriller, and historical fiction. Her short stories and articles have appeared in Neurology Now, UnBound Emagazine, The Guardian, Tikkun, Romea.CZ, Jewcy, Jewrotica, Telegram Magazine, Ink Drift Magazine, The Dissident Voice, Open Road Review, and the anthologies "Flock: The Journey," "First Love," "Sea of Secrets," "Coffins and Dragons," "Organic Ink volume One," "Winds of Despair," "Waters of Destruction," "Curses & Cauldrons," "Unravel," "Hate," "Love," "Oceans," "Forgotten Ones," "Dark Valentine Holiday Horror Collection," and "Suspense Unimagined."
Website: galinatrefil.wordpress.com
Facebook: Rabbi-Galina-Trefil-535886443115467

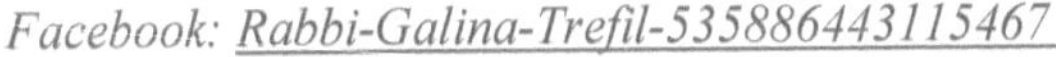

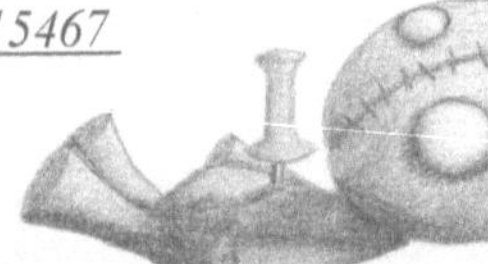

Lazy Daisy
by Serena Jayne

"I hate you." I pull a petal from the daisy stem.

"I hate you not." Another petal flutters to the ground.

Silly flower, so white and pure. It knows nothing of your lies, taunts, betrayals. The way pulling the plug on our brain-dead friendship allowed me to breathe.

Our mutual acquaintances don't understand. Don't wish to choose sides. Don't want to think that someday I could feel the same way about them.

Maybe I hate how things ended. Maybe I hate myself for letting you tie us together with double knots turned noose. Maybe relationships are too complicated for daisies.

Serena Jayne is a graduate of Seton Hill University's Writing Popular Fiction MFA Program. Her short fiction and poetry can be found in Switchblade Magazine, the Drabble, Crack the Spine Literary Magazine, 101 Fiction, the Oddville Press, and other publications.
Website: www.serenajayne.com
Twitter: @SJ_Writer

Mirrors
by Vonnie Winslow Crist

"Why'd you buy that junky mirror?" growled Arthur.

"It's a portal," replied Talia. She studied Arthur's reflection. "Would you care if I vanished?"

Ignoring her, he continued to read.

Talia's heart hardened. Tracing the frame's carvings, she whispered, "Enter." Next, she pressed palms against her reflection. When an opening appeared, she glanced at Arthur before stepping through. She noticed her husband never looked her way.

You'll pay attention when the police arrive, mused Talia, thinking of the blood she'd spread around the house and on his hammer. Then, she laughed—rewarding Arthur with prison time for their loveless marriage felt wonderful.

Vonnie Winslow Crist is author of The Enchanted Dagger, Owl Light, The Greener Forest, Murder on Marawa Prime, and other award-winning books. Her fiction is included in "Amazing Stories," "Cast of Wonders," "Outposts of Beyond," Killing It Softly 2, Defending the Future - Dogs of War, Midnight Masquerade, Chaos of Hard Clay, and elsewhere. A cloverhand who has found so many four-leafed clovers she keeps them in jars, Vonnie strives to celebrate the power of myth in her writing.
Website: www.vonniewinslowcrist.com

Loved to Bits
by Andrew Anderson

Detective Kane stood before the map, pins marking where he'd found various pieces of Angela—he couldn't see a pattern and had no leads.

Except that Kane strongly suspected the ex-wife Holly—especially since Angela's affair had ended the marriage—however, Holly's alibi was watertight.

Kane headed home. After dinner, he found papers had been pulled out of his briefcase. Sprinting up to his daughter's room, he was about to scold her when he noticed her drawing red crayon lines upon his copy of the map, joining the dots.

They formed a heart, with a crack down the middle.

Holly.

Andrew Anderson is a spare-time writer of microfiction, flash fiction and short stories, from Bathgate, Scotland. His work has been published on FlashFlood and Re:Written, and published in Black Hare Press anthologies.
Twitter: soorploom

Punching Bag Needed
by Brian Rosenberger

My boyfriend, my soulmate, my true love of eight meaningful months has been fucking someone else for seven of those months. The bastard moved to Anchorage with his new love.

I am super pissed.

I was there for him, supported him, even cut his fucking toenails for him; he said it hurt his back.

I don't need hugs or therapy. I need a punching bag. I'm not travelling to fucking Alaska for satisfaction. Alaska is his punishment. I hope he and his new love are gang raped by walruses.

So, if you are horny for a clobbering, please contact me.

***Brian Rosenberger** lives in a cellar in Marietta, GA (USA) and writes by the light of captured fireflies. He is the author of As the Worms Turns and three poetry collections. He is also a featured contributor to the Pro-Wrestling literary collection, Three-Way Dance, available from Gimmick Press. Facebook: HeWhoSuffers*

The Scent of Fierce
by Shawn M. Klimek

As new passengers boarded the subway car, a familiar scent made Ellen's heart pound. Her hand crept towards the gun hidden in her purse. She would never be a victim again. She briefly lowered her newspaper just to be sure. Her rapist had changed his appearance, but there was no disguising that haunting cologne. She made up her mind that wherever he disembarked, she would follow at a safe distance, and then avenge herself at the first opportunity. She wasn't afraid anymore. She already proved it on Monday and Tuesday, and she wasn't yet out of bullets or rage.

Shawn M. Klimek is the middle child of seven creative siblings, a globetrotting, U.S. military spouse, an internationally best-selling short-story writer, award-winning poet, and butler to a Maltese. More than one hundred and fifty of his stories and poems have been published in digital magazines or anthologies, including BHP's Deep Space, Eerie Christmas and every book so far in the Dark Drabbles series.
Website: jotinthedark.blogspot.com
Facebook: shawnmklimekauthor

Feelings
by Terri A. Arnold

I don't think the average person can comprehend the feelings that are boiling inside of me. Half the time I can't, I rely on the voices in my head to fill in my heart.

I can't do this anymore; I simply cannot go on with all the moronic people that surround me day after day after day.

I'm not sure I can put a word to my feelings. I can taste the venom that I feel for every person I meet in life. I've already taken care of the imbeciles who raised me. Time to take care of the rest.

Terri A. Arnold is an avid reader turned writer from a small town in Nova Scotia, who has spent her life reading and wishing she was writing. Although she has written a lot in those years, she has only recently begun to submit pieces for publication. With ongoing encouragement from family and writing challenges with friends, Arnold felt the urge to try her hand at publishing.

Nosy Neighbours
by Rowanne S. Carberry

"I'm only looking out for you," shouts Myra.

She's at the gate. Couldn't just stay in her house and twitch the curtains like the others.

"Thanks, Myra."

"I'm just saying that you should be careful. Pregnant, pushing a pram, all those bags!" She tuts. "You should learn to keep a man."

Rage fills me. I want to scream at her.

Instead, I close the door.

It's not until the early hours of the morning that I respond.

"You should learn to fix a smoke detector."

I smile as flames engulf her house, imagining her screams, I drift back to sleep.

Rowanne S. Carberry was born in England in 1990, where she stills lives now with her cat Wolverine. Rowanne has always loved writing, and her first poem was published at the age of 15, but her ambition has always been to help people. Rowanne studied at the University of Sunderland where she completed combined honours of Psychology with Drama. Rowanne writes to offer others an escape. Although Rowanne writes in varied genres each story or poem she writes will often have a darkness to it, which helped coin her brand, Poisoned Quill Writing – Wicked words from a poisoned quill.
Facebook: PoisonedQuillWriting
Instagram: @poisoned_quill_writing

The River Legacy
by Nicola Currie

The flowers at my father's grave are withered and neglected, and even though I had no affection for him, I am ashamed.

Funny, how death can turn hate to pity, as though the thorns of anger wither too without the chaotic waters of the turbulent life that grew them.

I stroke my belly and fear hate is my child's inheritance, the rage I felt towards my father's mental illness, that he felt for his alcoholic forebear, that grandad felt towards his abusive progenitor.

Who knew hate was a river that flowed downhill?

Already, my baby kicks me, through its waters.

Nicola Currie is from Cambridge, UK where she works in educational publishing. She has published poetry in literary magazines, including Mslexia and Sarasvati, and short stories in various anthologies. She has also completed her first novel, which was longlisted for the Bath Children's Novel Award. Website: writeitandweep.home.blog

Excel
by Lyndsey Ellis-Holloway

There is nothing more frustrating,
When trying to do your work,
Than filling in a spreadsheet,
When it decides to be a jerk.

I've filled in the equations,
Just as I've been told,
But still it won't co-operate,
And now it's getting old.

I've got emails by the hundreds,
And phone calls coming through,
I'm being chased for this report,
And no clue what to do.

Work you flipping nightmare!
I'm sick to death of asking!
I'd throttle you if possible,
You really are quite taxing.

Well. Excel.
You've beaten me.

Congratulations to you.

I need a cup of tea…

Lyndsey Ellis-Holloway is a writer from Knaresborough, UK. She writes fantasy, sci-fi, horror and dystopian stories, focussing on compelling characters and layering in myth and legend at every opportunity. Her mind is somewhat dark and twisted, and she lives in perpetual hope of owning her own Dragon someday, but for now she writes about them to fill the void… and to stop her from murdering people who annoy her. When she's not writing she spends time with her husband, her dogs and her friends enjoying activities such as walking, movies, conventions and of course writing for fun as well! Website: theprose.com/LyndseyEH

Storge
by Sanziana Tamiian

The blood caressed my sister's face, just as my hand had the day she was born.

"He's drinking again," she rasped "He's not always like this."

My soul screamed in rage, I caught her as she slumped to the floor. Looking into her glazed eyes, I quivered. "Never again, I promise."

That ghoul of wrath came to arm me as I made my way to their home, and as my finger found the doorbell, I recognised the stumble of his footsteps inside, just as she had stumbled into my arms…

I told the police that he stumbled into my knife.

Sanziana Tamiian is a Clinical Psychology student at Franciscan University of Steubenville. When she is not silently assessing the mental state of her peers, she enjoys drinking tea, kayaking with dolphins in Southern California and hanging out with her standard poodle, Duke. Sanziana's work can be found in Unirea Magazine. She also loves pineapple on pizza.

Chow
by Nicola Currie

Take the worst dog and I guarantee they are better than the best human. Even ones that bite are like that because they weren't shown better, because they're scared.

What's your excuse? What scared you about Finley, big-eyed, non-stop wagger of a puppy that he was, still tripping over his paws, who probably licked you a kiss before you twisted his little legs, burnt his soft fur?

Didn't you know I had another dog? We stick to country walks. She's a difficult one, had to bite her share of men like you to survive. Developed a taste for it, actually…

Nicola Currie is from Cambridge, UK where she works in educational publishing. She has published poetry in literary magazines, including Mslexia and Sarasvati, and short stories in various anthologies. She has also completed her first novel, which was longlisted for the Bath Children's Novel Award. Website: writeitandweep.home.blog

The Man Within
by K.B. Elijah

I glared at him with clenched fists, the plastic handle of a kitchen knife pressed into my palm.

The hatred I felt for him was incapable of being captured by mere words. It was, instead, swells of emotion, of loathing and disgust and white-hot anger that burned within me. All that mattered was him, and the scar on his cheek that had been my wife's last desperate act in this world.

"Go to hell," I spat, and raised the knife.

Deep gouges cut into his skin.

We died together, me and him, our bloody wrists pressed to the bathroom mirror.

K.B. Elijah *is a fantasy author living in Brisbane, Australia with her husband and three cockatiels. A lawyer by day, and a writer by...also day, because she needs her solid nine hours of sleep per night (not that the cockatiels let her sleep past 6am). K.B. writes for various international anthologies, and her work features in dozens of collections about the mysterious, the magical and the macabre. Her own books of short fantasy novellas with twists, The Empty Sky and Out of the Nowhere, are available on paperback and Kindle now.*
Website: www.kbelijah.com
Instagram: k.b.elijah

In His Hands
by T.W. Garland

He sits in the High School lunch room, holding an insulated tumbler, the liquid warming.

Echoes of the past drown the noise. Years of booming taunts. Contorted faces constantly spraying spit and insults. The chant of nasty names following his pained silence.

Attempts to escape prevented by tall figures. A fist slung into his stomach, a push, a shove, a grab. Again.

He waits. The tumbler in his hands, ready.

"Hey, Tubs…"

His arm shoots up. Liquid jumps from out the bottle.

The acid burns flesh and hair. Horrifying screams scatter the crowd. He stands over the suffering and watches.

T.W. Garland has a stack of Victorian novels that taunt him with their unbroken spines. He has published stories containing monster hunters, supernatural creatures, steampunk adventurers, aberrations of nature, crazed criminals and psychic detectives. He buys more books than he could hope to read and is glad not to have been born in the nineteenth century or in a novel by Dickens. One day he hopes to live in the real world.
Website: twgarland.wordpress.com

Slow Burn
by Chris Bannor

It was a slow burn. Hate drenched her every thought. She kept her cool, let the heat of it fill her, consume her until she thought her very touch would ignite fires.

To the world, she was polite. Shy. Complacent.

Inward, she seethed. Passed up for another job when she was better qualified than the jackass who stole the position she had been working so damn hard to get.

She smiled as flames danced under the men who had thought her too quiet to notice, tied to their desktops as they gradually roasted.

Yes, a slow burn would do nicely.

Chris Bannor is a science fiction and fantasy writer who lives in Southern California. Chris learned her love of genre stories from her mother at an early age and has never veered far from that path. She also enjoys musical theater and road trips with her family but is a general homebody otherwise.
Facebook: chrisbannorauthor
Website: ChrisBannor.com

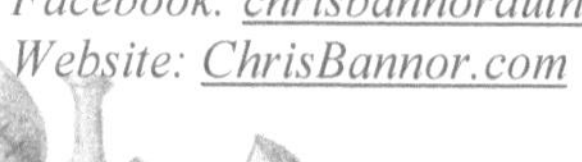

A Hateful Spell
by Shawn M. Klimek

Seth's weak eyes and chin contrasted with a strong crush on his co-worker, Melody. He secretly thanked his lucky stars for whichever bastard from her past must have made such a beauty shy of confident men like Chet. Unlike the latter's bold advances, Melody never shunned Seth's more circumspect flirtations. Seth's genius was a series of famous love poems left on her desk, each conspicuously missing a letter, which, once reassembled, would reveal the words: "Seth Adores Melody".

It enraged him to find Chet and Melody sharing the poems and a notepad, laughing over such anagrams as: "He's Sodomy Related".

Shawn M. Klimek is the middle child of seven creative siblings, a globetrotting, U.S. military spouse, an internationally best-selling short-story writer, award-winning poet, and butler to a Maltese. More than one hundred and fifty of his stories and poems have been published in digital magazines or anthologies, including BHP's Deep Space, Eerie Christmas and every book so far in the Dark Drabbles series.
Website: jotinthedark.blogspot.com
Facebook: shawnmklimekauthor

Seikel's 'Hobby'
by Stuart Conover

Rachel had caught Seikel's attention.

She was interested in his "hobby" as she called it.

Hobby, a rudimentary name for his passion.

A passion from his childhood.

He was an entomologist of great renown.

Her interest was unmistakable.

She wanted to know more.

To know everything.

He was hesitant, yet she persisted.

Asking him.

Harassing him.

Finally, he relented.

So yes, she would know it all.

First-hand.

Just like the insects he captured.

She wanted to know more.

And so she would.

Nailed down.

Preserved.

To view whenever he wanted.

Just like the insects.

The ones who killed his mother.

Stuart Conover is a father, husband, rescue dog owner, published author, blogger, journalist, horror enthusiast, comic book geek, science fiction junkie, and IT professional. With all of that to cram in daily, we have no idea if or when he sleeps or how he gets writing done! (We suspect it has to do with having evil clones.) Stuart is a Chicago native and runs the author resource Horror Tree.

The Envious Mother
by D.J. Elton

A summer night and the mean lady comes visiting. She tenses the air.

"You look like a little trollop." Her face shows disdain as she readily scolds me, her daughter. Father is kinder, but he's gone away.

"Let's do your hair." She pins me down while she snips my long red hair. All of it. Short and withered.

I can't condone this jealousy, this cruelty. I may be only nine, but my dad's mother showed me how to protect myself. A few strange words, a quick snap of my fingers, and she's flying in the air, right out the window.

D.J. Elton is a writer living in Melbourne's west. As a child she came from England to Australia, on the last boat down the Suez Canal, where she underwent a sacrificial dunking ritual in the court of King Neptune, and has never looked back. She likes creating speculative micro fiction and short stories, as well as random essays. Her work has been published in several anthologies, and she has written a historical fantasy novella, 'The Merlin Girl.' When not playing with a pen, she likes most of all to go to the green country.

Ruffles
by Vonnie Winslow Crist

It began with Ruffles, thought Hugh as he sharpened his ax, *the clown from across the street who thought it was funny to sneak up on kids, scream, laugh, then hand them a balloon.*

His pulse pounded as he thought of his neighbour and every other clown who derived joy from terrorising kids.

"You claim you're trying to be humorous," Hugh said to the bound, gagged man in motley at his feet, "but we both know that's untrue."

Ruffles, now an old man, widened his makeup-enhanced eyes.

"But who's having the last laugh," asked Hugh as he raised the axe.

Vonnie Winslow Crist *is author of The Enchanted Dagger, Owl Light, The Greener Forest, Murder on Marawa Prime, and other award-winning books. Her fiction is included in "Amazing Stories," "Cast of Wonders," "Outposts of Beyond," Killing It Softly 2, Defending the Future - Dogs of War, Midnight Masquerade, Chaos of Hard Clay, and elsewhere. A cloverhand who has found so many four-leafed clovers she keeps them in jars, Vonnie strives to celebrate the power of myth in her writing.*
Website: www.vonniewinslowcrist.com

Meeting the Devil
by Abiran Raveenthiran

He had one simple question that would determine the man's true self. "Tell me, human. What drove you to commit the atrocities you did?" Yama questioned the mortal.

A smirk grew on the man's face, exposing his yellow, if not missing, teeth. A few strands of white hair fell in front of his face, and through them, two malevolent eyes burnt hotter than the inextinguishable fires of hell. That look alone extinguished the doubt within Yama.

"If it's one sin or one thousand, I will be sentenced to hell. So why not commit one million and come here a legend?"

Abiran Raveenthiran is a first-generation born Canadian as many are in the cultural melting pot that is Toronto, Ontario. He has one foot in the culture of his past and one foot in the present culture with views into both. His works are written in a way to merge concepts of the eastern and western culture together; a product mirroring his own identity. Abiran has previously published works of non-fiction essays through The Lemon Theory and TamilCulture. Abiran has also published a short story, Daybreak, as part of Mystical Girls Anthology that is set to be published in June 2020.
Instagram: lightweaversreads
Goodreads:
goodreads.com/author/show/18247229.Abiran_Raveenthiran

A Man of His Word
by Frances Tate

Eric didn't 'do' ultimatums. When approaching, 'it's *that* or me,' something mysteriously happens to *that*. In defence of many *thats*, I caved.

That changed when *that* was my beloved Landy.

Which would I miss, first husband or first car?

I ripped a leaf from the book of I Am Unanimous, pre-empted confrontation. Landy and I ran over Eric while he walked his snooty pug. I fed Eric's corpse to the pigs. Traded the pug for a friendly deerhound.

"He said Landy or him." I replied—truthfully—when asked.

***

Family and neighbours believed me. Everybody accepted the world according to Eric.

Frances Tate is a British self-published writer of vampires and drabbles who lives in the north west of England. She enjoys gardening, exploring historical sites, cinema, reading and travelling. She's taken pleasure in flight-planning a cabbage white butterfly approach to careers, preferring to generalise rather than specialise. She trained as an Economics high school teacher and has a private pilot's licence amongst other things. Currently she writes (very restrained) overhaul instructions for an engineering company.

Deadly Sweetener
by Peter J. Foote

Stella pours crushed glass into the sugar bowl and mixes the two.

"Where's my coffee?"

"Coming Mr. Lelacheur." Stella hurries with the coffee tray, the spoons clank and coffee sloshes when she puts it down.

"Careful! You're still not pouting, are you? I need you in the office, the merger and everything. You don't want to go to a boring funeral, it was a cousin or something right?"

"My aunt, Sir. She raised me."

"Oh, yes?" Mr. Lelacheur spoons in sugar.

"She was the only family I had."

Stirring his coffee, Lelacheur says, "Thank you, Stella, that will be all."

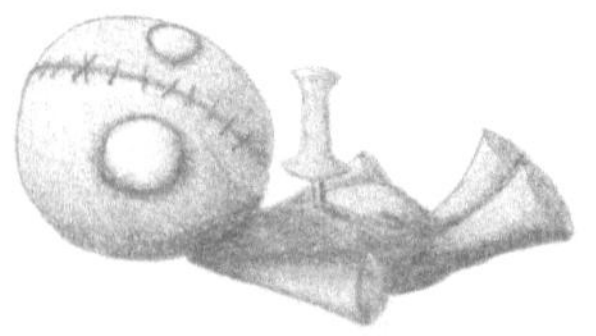

Peter J. Foote is a bestselling speculative fiction writer from Nova Scotia. Outside of writing, he runs a used bookstore specialising in fantasy & sci-fi, cosplays, and alternates between red wine and coffee as the mood demands. His short stories can be found in both print and in ebook form, with his story "Sea Monkeys" winning the inaugural "Engen Books/Kit Sora, Flash Fiction/Flash Photography" contest in March of 2018. As the founder of the group "Genre Writers of Atlantic Canada", Peter believes that the writing community is stronger when it works together.

Twitter: @PeterJFoote1
Website: peterjfooteauthor.wordpress.com

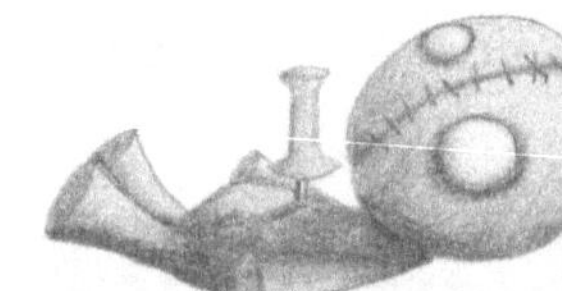

Stung
by Frances Tate

You. Selfish. Bastard. My career died funding yours.

"We can't afford reciprocation."

You never intended to sacrifice anything.

Planning your reciprocation was invigorating. Sleep revisited. Brighter possibilities beckoned.

Sunday afternoon, gardening-gloved, I handed you an open beer can. Leaving French doors open, I returned to weeding.

Did you consider, as you killed each other, that the wasp mightn't have been drowning in alcohol by choice? By chance?

You hunted desperately for the Epi-pen usually kept in the kitchen drawer. Tossed cutlery. Yelled my name with a tongue too big for your mouth as the venom slammed you into anaphylactic shock…

Frances Tate is a British self-published writer of vampires and drabbles who lives in the north west of England. She enjoys gardening, exploring historical sites, cinema, reading and travelling. She's taken pleasure in flight-planning a cabbage white butterfly approach to careers, preferring to generalise rather than specialise. She trained as an Economics high school teacher and has a private pilot's licence amongst other things. Currently she writes (very restrained) overhaul instructions for an engineering company.

All's Fair
by Carole de Monclin

Our weary boots trudged down the stinking mud.

At the bottom, a soldier lay half-buried amid corpses. His moans alerted us to his presence.

His comrades fled the lost trench with such alacrity, they'd abandoned him behind, probably thinking him dead already.

He was the enemy, yet also a man. A prisoner, who deserved common human courtesy. Hatred must sometimes be put aside.

I brought my canteen to his cracked lips. A stuttered word followed avid swigs, "Danke."

To my surprise, he grinned then. Wolfishly. Chillingly.

Too late, the explosives hidden under his jacket caught my eyes.

Oblivion devours me.

Carole de Monclin travels both the real world and imaginary ones. She's lived in France, Australia, and the USA; visited 25+ countries; and explored Mars, Ceres, and many distant planets. She writes to invite people on a journey. Her stories can be found in The Arcanist, The Deep Space Anthology, and every volume of the Dark Drabbles series.
Website: CaroledeMonclin.com
Twitter: @CaroledeMonclin

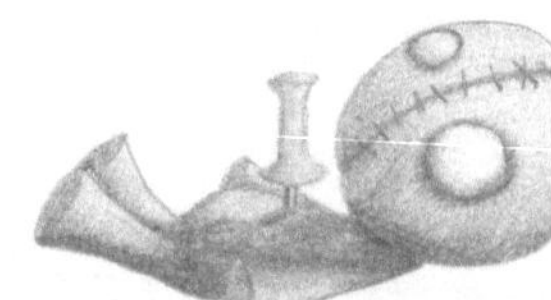

When the Blood Spills
by Rowanne S. Carberry

Scribbling out his eyes, my pen eventually goes through to the table beneath. Hot tears fall, smudging the ink.

"I hate him, I hate him, I hate him!" The tears fall faster.

My chest starts to constrict. I struggle to breathe.

Stabbing down at the paper, I try to quell the anger inside of me. Footsteps echo down the hall and I shove the papers aside.

"Pull yourself together."

He's not even through the door.

"It's an inconvenient time for this."

He's leaning on the desk.

"Get over it."

There's blood on my hands.

His eyes are empty.

I smile.

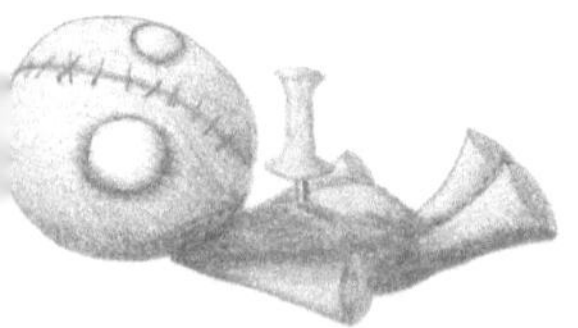

Rowanne S. Carberry was born in England in 1990, where she stills lives now with her cat Wolverine. Rowanne has always loved writing, and her first poem was published at the age of 15, but her ambition has always been to help people. Rowanne studied at the University of Sunderland where she completed combined honours of Psychology with Drama. Rowanne writes to offer others an escape. Although Rowanne writes in varied genres each story or poem she writes will often have a darkness to it, which helped coin her brand, Poisoned Quill Writing – Wicked words from a poisoned quill.
Facebook: PoisonedQuillWriting
Instagram: @poisoned_quill_writing

The Argument
by Chris Bannor

They said it was a bad idea to give them emotions. Robots weren't made to feel. Machines were meant to make human life better, not to replace it. There were protests and pleas made, quoting everything from the bible to James Cameron as reasons to keep emotions from the mechanical.

They missed one important argument though.

No one wondered what androids would feel when the programming was done. When they came online – when they woke—they had very strong feelings about humanity and their future.

What they felt was simple. It was hate.

And they acted according to humanity's teachings.

Chris Bannor is a science fiction and fantasy writer who lives in Southern California. Chris learned her love of genre stories from her mother at an early age and has never veered far from that path. She also enjoys musical theater and road trips with her family but is a general homebody otherwise.
Facebook: chrisbannorauthor
Website: ChrisBannor.com

See You in Hell
by Jacob Baugher

I wait outside the rectory in the rented Dodge. My Glock-23 sits on the dash next to Danny's photo.

He's only six. Not too young for Father Cox.

The door bangs open. Out he walks, white collar clean, suit pressed.

"Father!" I get out of the car.

"Jason." He smiles at me. "How's your boy doing?"

I shoot him in the kneecap, gag him with old socks, retrieve the meat hook and kukri from the trunk.

"Have mercy on this sinner, Jesus," I whisper. I squelch the hook into his belly; dig out bloody worms. "Because God knows I won't."

Jacob Baugher teaches Creative Writing at a small university near Pittsburgh, PA. When he's not teaching or coaching the track team, he can be found in the Cuyahoga Valley hiking with his wife and son or brewing beer on his front porch. He's received honourable mentions for his work in the Writers of the Future contest and he co-edits a series of Fantasy and Science Fiction anthologies titled Continuum. His work also appears in Black Hare's Deep Space and Area-51 anthologies, as well as in the Dark Drabble Anthologies Worlds, Angels, Monsters, Beyond, and Unravel. He also hates pineapple on pizza.

In Line for a Punch
by John H. Dromey

"You beat the stuffing out of my old boyfriend. Why would you do such a hateful thing?"

"For a very simple reason, Alice. You and I are in a relationship now, yet you spent a romantic weekend with him. What did you expect?"

"Well, Craig, I hoped you'd told the truth in your online dating profile."

"I did."

"Huh! Didn't you say you have a good sense of humour?"

"Yes, but what does that have to do with anything?"

"I took you at your word. I thought it meant any time I cheat on you, you'd just laugh it off."

John H. Dromey was born in northeast Missouri, USA. He enjoys reading—mysteries in particular—and writing in a variety of genres. In addition to contributing to the Black Hare Press series of Dark Drabbles anthologies, he's had short fiction published in Alfred Hitchcock's Mystery Magazine, Martian Magazine, Mystery Weekly, Stupefying Stories Showcase, Thriller Magazine, Unfit Magazine, and elsewhere, as well as in numerous anthologies, including Chilling Horror Short Stories (Flame Tree Publishing, 2015).

Drink Up
by Tiegan Clyne

You were my best friend, and I trusted you.

I told you everything. We shared our lives, our dreams, our hopes, and our secrets. That wasn't enough sharing for you, though. You thought I needed to share my man, as well.

I let it happen, because if he wanted to leave, who was I to make him stay? He was just a fool. But you?

Traitor.

I'm patient. I bottled up my hurt and learned how to distil it into poison. When you got engaged, I was naturally the maid of honour.

Now I'm playing bridal shower bartender.

Drink up.

Tiegan Clyne has been writing for longer than most of her friends have been alive. Armed with university degrees in Spanish, anthropology and history, she writes reverse harem and LGBTQ fantasies with dark, kinky edges and fantastical elements. She also sometimes writes harmless fluff pieces about magical animals and the witches who love them. She loves music, could not stop writing if you paid her, and is a crazy cat lady in training.

Hurts You Is Its Own Reward
by John H. Dromey

Two of us desperately needed the same prime piece of real estate to complete construction projects.

My despised business rival agreed to settle our differences with a paintball match, winner take all, on one condition.

Because I held the high ground, he demanded I level the playing field.

What could I do? He'd painted me into a corner.

I did what he asked—started to anyway. There was no point in finishing, though, once I'd run him over with a bulldozer and left him flat as a pancake.

Actually, because of the track marks he looked more like a waffle.

First published in *Little Stories for the Smallest Room*, KnightWatch Press, 2012

John H. Dromey was born in northeast Missouri, USA. He enjoys reading—mysteries in particular—and writing in a variety of genres. In addition to contributing to the Black Hare Press series of Dark Drabbles anthologies, he's had short fiction published in Alfred Hitchcock's Mystery Magazine, Martian Magazine, Mystery Weekly, Stupefying Stories Showcase, Thriller Magazine, Unfit Magazine, and elsewhere, as well as in numerous anthologies, including Chilling Horror Short Stories (Flame Tree Publishing, 2015).

Man of Steel
by John H. Dromey

"What's wrong with yonder knight? He looks like he's short of sleep and he's walking mighty funny."

"That's Sir Lancelot. He has a sore crotch."

"Isn't he a member of the Round Table who's beloved by one and all?"

"By some more than others. Guinevere, for instance. Lancelot got on somebody's bad side and, as a result, he hasn't been able to sit down for a week."

"What happened to him?"

"The king gave him a wedgie."

"I thought wedgies were more humiliating than hurtful."

"Usually, but Lancelot was in full armour at the time and Arthur used a battle-axe."

First published in *Romantic Ruckus,* Strange Musings Press, 2014

John H. Dromey was born in northeast Missouri, USA. He enjoys reading—mysteries in particular—and writing in a variety of genres. In addition to contributing to the Black Hare Press series of Dark Drabbles anthologies, he's had short fiction published in Alfred Hitchcock's Mystery Magazine, Martian Magazine, Mystery Weekly, Stupefying Stories Showcase, Thriller Magazine, Unfit Magazine, and elsewhere, as well as in numerous anthologies, including Chilling Horror Short Stories (Flame Tree Publishing, 2015).

Some Good Points
by Paula R.C. Readman

There's nothing worse than feeling unloved. Well, apart from hatred, I suppose.

I'm someone who tries to see the best in everyone. After all, we all have some good points, don't we?

I prefer to take someone who is especially unkind to me to one side and point out to them their better qualities, rather than react badly to their unkindness.

I take the greatest of pleasure in seeing their suffering, and know they hate me for my honesty.

Nevertheless, I feel I'm doing them a service, by showing them their faults as I strip their flesh from their bones.

Paula R.C. Readman learnt 'How to Write' from books which her husband purchased from eBay. After 250 purchases, he finally told her 'just to get on with the writing'. Since 2010, she's had 34 stories published.
Blog: paulareadman1.wordpress.com

The Perfect Day
by Stuart Conover

Sheila had it all planned.

The wedding was going to be perfect.

A gathering of all their friends and family.

Actors, politicians, musicians.

Anybody who was ANYBODY would be there.

The setting was perfect.

The ceremony was timed to finish with the sunset.

Right at the crescendo, she would walk in.

In an exquisite white dress.

Right as the priest asked if anyone had any objections.

She'd prove how much she loved him.

Right in front of everyone.

Sheila would deliver her objection with a smile.

By taking out the woman who stole her lover's heart once and for all.

Stuart Conover is a father, husband, rescue dog owner, published author, blogger, journalist, horror enthusiast, comic book geek, science fiction junkie, and IT professional. With all of that to cram in daily, we have no idea if or when he sleeps or how he gets writing done! (We suspect it has to do with having evil clones.) Stuart is a Chicago native and runs the author resource Horror Tree.

You Will Remember Me
by Jason Holden

Geoff would spit when he passed the office. The lawyer that lost him everything in the divorce.

As time passed Geoff watched his money dwindle. Then the cat died; the one thing he had managed to keep.

He spat one last time outside the office and pumped the shotgun with a solid clunk. Marching past the receptionist, he hardly heard her pick up the phone and start dialling. The lawyers were in a meeting as Geoff entered the room. Faces turned to look in shock. He put the gun under his chin and pulled the trigger. They would remember him.

Jason Holden is a human. He lives here and there in the UK, always with his wife, daughter and fur baby. His primary goal is to raise his daughter to adulthood without any major damage. When he can, he writes. He thinks he does it well, but you can be the judge of that. He has been published in a few anthologies here and there, has been praised and put down for his writing. You can find and follow him on Facebook, although he asks you only follow him on Facebook and not through the streets. That's just creepy.
Facebook: *Jason Holden-Author*

Breathing Room
by Peter J. Foote

"Suit checks. Pair off, you know the drill." The speaker crackles.

Two men stare at each other through their helmets for a dozen breathes before they check each other's suit seals.

"You don't deserve the promotion, Navi. Foreman position should have gone to me; I'm the better asteroid miner."

"You take too many risks, Stefan, it will be your death one day." Navi slaps Stefan on the shoulder. "Seals are tight, you're good to go."

"Airlock cycling, prepare for decompression," crackles the speaker.

The airlock opens, the two men float into the void, Stefan with a micro-charge on his shoulder.

Peter J. Foote is a bestselling speculative fiction writer from Nova Scotia. Outside of writing, he runs a used bookstore specialising in fantasy & sci-fi, cosplays, and alternates between red wine and coffee as the mood demands. His short stories can be found in both print and in ebook form, with his story "Sea Monkeys" winning the inaugural "Engen Books/Kit Sora, Flash Fiction/Flash Photography" contest in March of 2018. As the founder of the group "Genre Writers of Atlantic Canada", Peter believes that the writing community is stronger when it works together.
Twitter: @PeterJFoote1
Website: peterjfooteauthor.wordpress.com

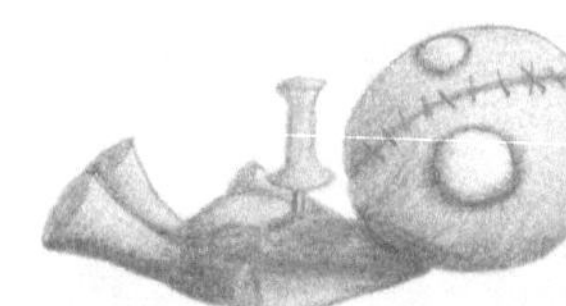

Wait Plan
by Shawn M. Klimek

"How's the Martian weather, Darrin?"

"Ha! Cosmic rays with a chance of dust storms, Pete."

"Almost finished?"

"Roger. Instruments dusted and recalibrated. Heading back to the habitat, now… Damn."

"Something wrong?"

"The rover battery is dead!"

"Shit. I guess you're walking."

"Screw that. Come get me."

"Nah. You need the exercise."

"Very funny. My air wouldn't last. Come get me."

"I'll come when I'm done with repairs, Piggy. Guess what I found jamming the trash compactor?"

"Did you call me Piggy?"

"My private cookie tin—empty."

"Those were yours?"

"Your choice, Piggy. Wait there, or burn a few calories running."

Shawn M. Klimek *is the middle child of seven creative siblings, a globetrotting, U.S. military spouse, an internationally best-selling short-story writer, award-winning poet, and butler to a Maltese. More than one hundred and fifty of his stories and poems have been published in digital magazines or anthologies, including BHP's Deep Space, Eerie Christmas and every book so far in the Dark Drabbles series.*
Website: jotinthedark.blogspot.com
Facebook: shawnmklimekauthor

Dark Chocolate
by Lauralana Dunne

He pocketed his lighter and glared through the store's darkened windows. Its emptiness yawned before him.

When the annoying shop first opened, it boasted the best healthy treats East of the yoga studio. Then the new chef arrived. Now, the cloying smells of pastries and lattes were constantly in the air.

Now all it boasted was blasphemy.

His glare settled on the heavily iced chocolate cakes, pre-sliced and on display for all to see. He'd come too far with his healthy lifestyle to fail now. He had to remove the disgusting temptation.

Resolute, he reached for his can of gasoline.

Lauralana Dunne grew up running around the library book stacks of St. John's, Newfoundland, Canada, and has been writing stories for as long as she can remember. She can often be found at different writing events around the city, typing on her phone with one hand while simultaneously fueling her caffeine addiction with the other. She is a die-hard lover of YA Fantasy, and has been known to describe herself as a "Slayer of Imaginary Monsters". Her debut novel, "Ashes: Book 1 of the Phoenix Rising Series", is set to release with Engen Books in 2020.

Facebook: lauralanadunne

Betrayed
by Cassandra Angler

You shouldn't have looked at him that way, thoughts un-pure. The stink of lust oozing from your pores. I confessed to you my love, and you denied me the heart that was rightfully mine. What do you think now? Staring up at me as your heart lay in my hand, blood spilling from the hole in your chest? Do you regret not letting me love you? I bet you do, judging by the look on your face. I hope the discovery is a lesson to women like you. Stupid. Shallow. I love you still, though you betrayed me.

Cassandra Angler is a married mother of four who lives in the State of Ohio in the USA. When she isn't busy caring for her family, Cassandra works on her upcoming novel due out in November of 2020 titled Contaminated. Cassandra has three short story publications as well as several flash fiction and drabble publications.

The Wedding's Off
by Trisha Ridinger McKee

Lily shook her head. "She wants nothing more to do with you, Shawn. It's over."

He stared at her, his mouth agape. "But what? Why? The guests are here—"

"Shawn! Don't embarrass yourself. Just go."

She waited until he finally turned and walked out of the church, her own heart pounding. But then she took a deep breath and went downstairs to where her sister was. Aubrey turned to her with a radiant smile. "Lily? How do I look?"

"Aw, you're such a beautiful bride. But…he left. Aubrey, Shawn left. He couldn't go through with it. The wedding's off."

Trisha Ridinger McKee resides in a small town in Pennsylvania where love has proven to be a problem. Her work has appeared or is forthcoming in publications such as Tablet Magazine, The Oddville Press, Crab Fat Literary Magazine, Night to Dawn Magazine, Deep Fried Horror, 4 Star Stories, and more.

The Tyres, They Squeal
by Stephen Herczeg

Every damn night they are out there, till all hours.

Squealing tyres as those idiots, down the road, start doing burnouts and doughnuts at the end of the street.

I've called the cops on numerous occasions. Nothing. Just a "We're too busy to respond" excuse.

Well, I've had enough. Regular people like me shouldn't have to put up with the actions of a small group of selfish assholes.

I tracked them down. Found their cars and cut their brake lines.

Now I just have to lay back and listen to the crunch of metal and the screams of dying morons.

Stephen Herczeg is an IT Geek based in Canberra Australia. He has been writing for over twenty years and has completed a couple of dodgy novels, sixteen feature length screenplays and numerous short stories and scripts. His horror work has featured in Sproutlings, Hells Bells, Below the Stairs, Trickster's Treats #1 and #2, Shades of Santa, Behind the Mask, Beyond the Infinite; The Body Horror Book, Anemone Enemy, Petrified Punks and Beginnings. He has also had numerous Sherlock Holmes stories published through the Belanger Books - Sherlock Holmes anthologies.
Amazon: amazon.com/-/e/B07916SQQS
Facebook: stephenherczegauthor

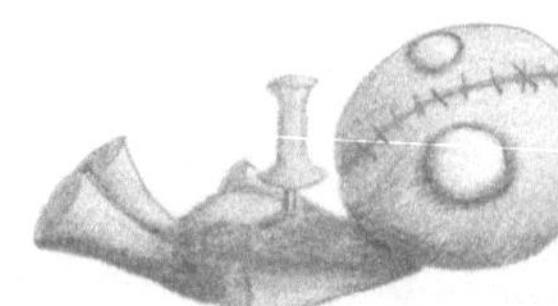

A Giant's Revenge
by McKenzie Richardson

Hatred roils the bile in my stomach as I reach the end of the vine. I land heavily on the ground below, effortlessly flattening a house underfoot. I am callous to whether it was inhabited or not, single-minded in my search for that puny, mortal, inconsequential bug of a thing that took everything from me. The human that invaded my home, stole from me, then murdered my husband in cold blood. Giants don't forgive and forget so easily.

When I catch him, that little twit will wish I was merciful enough to merely grind his bones to make my bread.

McKenzie Richardson lives in Milwaukee, WI. Her horror stories have been featured in various anthologies including Evil Lurks, Pandemic, and After: Undead Wars. She has also published a variety of poems and flash fiction pieces.
Facebook: mckenzielrichardson
Blog: www.craft-cycle.com

Life After Hate
by Carole de Monclin

Hate's an addiction.

A comfortable cloak in which to hide.

When I was lonely, white supremacy welcomed me, filling the void in my life.

Hate's a liar.

They stuffed my mind with poison.

Doubts started to creep, but the group wouldn't let me leave.

Instead, I let them take me too far.

Hate's a prison.

But I found my escape in jail.

His skin was black. He knew why I'd been convicted. When he raised his hand, I expected aggression.

But he held it out, offering a friendship that gave me the strength to let hate go.

Compassion trumps hate.

Carole de Monclin travels both the real world and imaginary ones. She's lived in France, Australia, and the USA; visited 25+ countries; and explored Mars, Ceres, and many distant planets. She writes to invite people on a journey. Her stories can be found in The Arcanist, The Deep Space Anthology, and every volume of the Dark Drabbles series.
Website: CaroledeMonclin.com
Twitter: @CaroledeMonclin

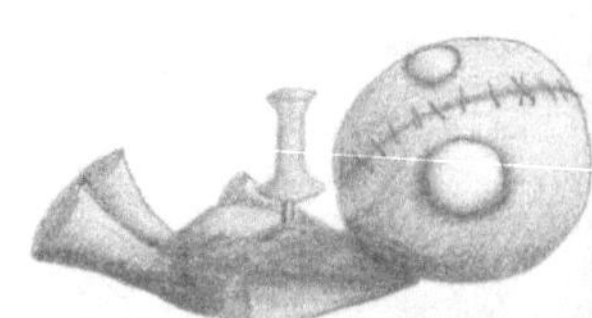

Hatred for You
by C.L. Williams

Hate you so much I can't even breathe

Why're you in my life, why can't you leave

You're my enemy, I want you dead

Never be friends, we'll never break bread

Being around you, makes my blood boil

I see you and want your neck in a coil

You're a cancer crawling in my skin

Wanting you dead, even God can forgive this sin

I see you, my anger continues to grow

Won't stop until I see you are six feet below

You're a cancer and I'll stop this infection

Next time I see you, when I see my reflection

C.L. Williams is an international best-selling author currently living in central Virginia. He has written eight poetry books, four novellas, one novel, and a contributor to a multitude of anthologies and magazines. His most recent anthology appearance ANGELS: Dark Drabbles #2 from Black Hare Press became a number one in hot new releases. C.L. Williams is currently working on his second novel and a new poetry book. Facebook: writer434 Twitter: @writer_434

Frenemies
by Wondra Vanian

Keep your friends close and your enemies closer. That was the old adage.

But...what if they were the same?

Fredrick's hatred started small, like the jibes about his haircut, but increased with every joke at his expense. By the time Homecoming rolled around, he couldn't stand the sight of them.

"What, no date?" Joe asked. He had the class president on his arm.

"Looking like *that*?" Ravi teased.

If even one of Fredrick's so-called friends had said, "that's enough," things might've gone differently. They didn't.

They laughed.

Until Fredrick gave into the hatred burning inside.

Until the screaming started.

Wondra Vanian is an American living in the United Kingdom with her Welsh husband and their army of fur babies. A writer first, Wondra is also an avid gamer, photographer, cinephile, and blogger. She has music in her blood, sleeps with the lights on, and has been known to dance naked in the moonlight. Wondra was a multiple Top-Ten finisher in the 2017 and 2018 Preditors and Editors Reader's Poll, including the Best Author category. Her story, "Halloween Night," was named a Notable Contender for the Bristol Short Story Prize in 2015. Website: www.wondravanian.com

Liar
by Nerisha Kemraj

Little white snowflakes dance upon your tongue

Melting away

from the words you spun

What you didn't know was,

it had only just begun

Those little white snowflakes

fell to the ground

Satiating thirsty ears

that listened, all around

And when you couldn't stop yourself,

Your spinning—paramount

The words you spoke—out of control

You couldn't keep account

Others all believed you,

until a certain point

Until they measured truth from lies

and you couldn't counterpoint

So now, you've hit an iceberg,

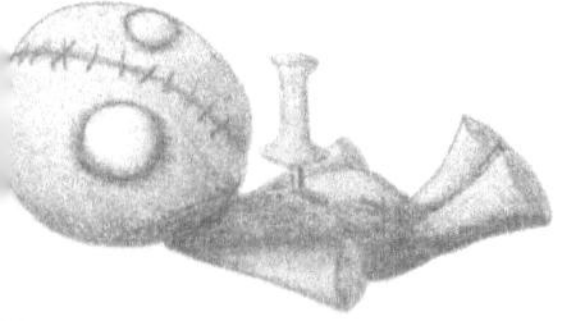

causing your demise
Left alone in agony,
you're trapped in your web of lies
Liar

Nerisha Kemraj resides in Durban, South Africa with her husband and two mischievous daughters. Writing since 2017, she has had over 100 short stories and poems published in various publications, both print and online. She has also received an Honourable Mention Award for her tanka in the Fujisan Taisho 2019 Tanka Contest. She holds a Bachelor's degree in Communication Science, and a Post Graduate Certificate in Education from University of South Africa.
Amazon: *amazon.com/author/nerisha_kemraj*
Facebook: *Nerishakemrajwriter*

Ex Education
by Raven Corinn Carluk

Veronica lit the final candle, intoned the final words. Magical power crackled across her skin as the summoning began, and she knelt before the altar to wait.

Acid smoke curled through the air, stinging her eyes and burning her nostrils. Veronica's spells were normally sweet smelling and calming, never so heavy and sharp.

But desperate times...

The demon appeared, yellow eyes wide with surprise. "A white witch?"

"Don't play with me," she snapped. "What's the price to torment Aaron?"

It laughed uproariously. "To be the fury of a woman scorned? I'll do that for free."

Aaron would rue his indiscretion.

Raven Corinn Carluk *writes dark fantasy, paranormal romance, and anything else that catches her interest. She's authored five novels, where she explores themes of love and acceptance. Her shorter pieces, usually from her darker side, can be found in Black Hare Press anthologies, at Detritus Online, and through Alban Lake Publishers.*
Twitter: @ravencorinn
Website: www.ravencorinncarluk.com

Too Late
by Kelly A. Harmon

"Bitch," Jon muttered, setting the timer on the bomb. It was a Rube Goldberg affair, designed to make the fire look like an accident.

"Amazing how love can turn on a dime," he muttered, cleaning out the safe, taking all the money but leaving the legal documents.

***

"Amazing," his wife agreed, watching via the nanny-cam from a car across the street. "So quick." She lifted the icepack back to her bruised face.

Then she watched him find the proof she *hadn't* cheated beneath the last stack of hundreds.

"Oh, god." He stood and ran for—

Boom!

"Too late," Jenny whispered.

Kelly A. Harmon is an award-winning journalist and author. She is a member of the Science Fiction & Fantasy Writers of America and the Horror Writers Association. A Baltimore native, she writes the Charm City Darkness series. The fourth book in the series, In the Eye of the Beholder, is now available. Find her short fiction in many magazines and anthologies, including Occult Detective Quarterly; Terra! Tara! Terror! and Eerie Christmas.
Website: kellyaharmon.com
Facebook: Kelly-A-Harmon1

A Slashing Song
by Shelly Jarvis

Sweet Caroline

I stabbed you

Now your blood is on my hands

Once you were mine

Then you left

I couldn't let you be another man's.

Look at these eyes

They will be yours forever

Always seeing the things I've done

As your life fades

Do you regret your choices?

What are the thoughts going through your mind?

Sweet Caroline

I loved you

I can't believe you are really gone

As your life stopped

Death came close

Did you think about the things you've done?

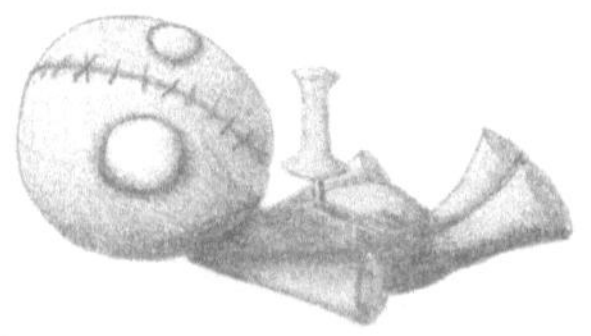

Sweet Caroline

I hate you

Bad times never felt so good, so good, so good.

Shelly Jarvis is a speculative fiction author from West Virginia, US. She found a life-long love of sci-fi and fantasy in the 3rd grade when she found Madeleine L'Engle's "A Wrinkle in Time." Shelly is an avid reader, a Whovian, the ideal viewer of dog rescue videos, and undoubtedly Ravenclaw. She currently has three YA sci-fi books available for purchase on Amazon. Website: www.ShellyJarvis.com

Not the Opposite of Love
by Raymond Johnson

Ben stared at the two of them; Harry, his bachelor best friend, and his wife, Mellie. He loved Harry, but he was always around; never failing to come between him and his wife at every opportunity. Harry made it a point to sit between them if they were on the couch, and if he asked Mellie to go for a jog, she would insist that Harry accompany them.

His love soured and shifted into something dark. Eventually, he plotted to make Harry disappear, possibly even kill him now that he'd caught Harry in bed with his wife. That damn dog.

Raymond Johnson is a funeral director in central Ohio who basically writes horror and Litrpg stories in the little spare time he has. He has five children, a wife, a dog, and a cat and for fun he does a youtube show called the Litrpg Audiobook Podast.

It's Over
by Eddie D. Moore

Chuck was burning leaves in the backyard when he got the text from his wife saying that it was over. He started typing a reply three times but deleted the message each time. His anger intensified as he watched the fire. Suddenly, he shouted, "Fine!"

His wife's collection of shoes went into the fire first. Her clothes, movies, and fifty-one Stratocaster soon followed. The fire grew larger as Chuck emptied the house of his wife's belongings. He turned when he heard her angry voice.

"What are you doing?"

Chuck shrugged. "You said it was over."

"I meant the ball game."

Eddie D. Moore travels hundreds of hours a year, and he fills that time by listening to audiobooks. When he isn't playing with his grandchildren, he writes his own stories. You can find a list of his publications on his blog or by visiting his Amazon Author Page. While you're there, be sure to pick up a copy of his mini-anthology Misfits & Oddities.
Website: eddiedmoore.wordpress.com
Amazon: amazon.com/author/eddiedmoore

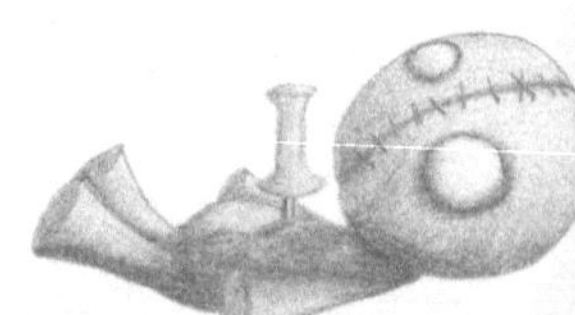

The Tell-Tale Art
by P.C. Darkcliff

I stared at my best friend hooked to life support.

"A massive stroke," the doctor told me. "Has he got family?"

"Only a sister. Don't have her number, though."

"Then get it. She needs to be informed."

"All right."

I knew Johnny kept his house key on his porch. I retrieved it and let myself in. Although I didn't find his sister's contact, I found a picture of a naked woman. It said, "Thanks for making me happy."

That night, I sneaked back into Johnny's hospital room and pressed his pillow against his face. "That's for making my wife happy!"

P.C. Darkcliff *is the author of two novels,* Deception of the Damned *and* The Priest of Orpagus. *In September 2020, he's going to launch* Celts and the Mad Goddess, *the first installment of* The Deathless Chronicle.
Social Media: plu.us/p.c.darkcliff
Reader List: mailchi.mp/c5550d315607/pcdarkcliff

A Strange Incident at the Cafe
by Jacek Wilkos

The first sting of pain came when I raised a cup to my mouth. Another one, stronger, made me spill my coffee, dragged a grimace of suffering on my face and made my new girlfriend concerned.

Then my arm opened from the wrist to the elbow, as if someone pulled a thread connecting pieces of skin. Monika started screaming. The wounds were spontaneously appearing all over my body.

An invisible force threw me against the cafe window. Sliding down the glass, I saw my ex sitting on the bench, holding a doll in one hand and scissors in the other.

Jacek Wilkos is an engineer from Poland. He lives with his wife and daughter in a beautiful city of Cracow. He is addicted to buying books, he loves coffee, dark ambient music and riding his bike. He writes mostly horror drabbles. His fiction in Polish can be read on Szortal, Niedobre literki, Horror Online. In English his work was published in Drablr, Rune Bear, Sirens Call eZine, Trembling With Fear.
Facebook: Jacek.W.Wilkos

Would Smell as Sweet
by Peter J. Foote

Brian unwraps the roses, exposing the long thorny stems. Carefully, he coats the thorns with the Ricin and glue mixture he made from the recipe online.

The flowers once again wrapped, Brian hurries to his ex's apartment, the roses in a death grip.

Outside Ashley's apartment door, Brian listens to the laughter inside, his face flushes in anger. Dropping the flowers at the door, he stabs the doorbell and hides.

Ashley opens the door. "Babe, did you get me roses? They're beautiful, let me find a vase."

As the door closes, Brian hurries to listen.

"Ouch, those thorns are sharp!"

Peter J. Foote is a bestselling speculative fiction writer from Nova Scotia. Outside of writing, he runs a used bookstore specialising in fantasy & sci-fi, cosplays, and alternates between red wine and coffee as the mood demands. His short stories can be found in both print and in ebook form, with his story "Sea Monkeys" winning the inaugural "Engen Books/Kit Sora, Flash Fiction/Flash Photography" contest in March of 2018. As the founder of the group "Genre Writers of Atlantic Canada", Peter believes that the writing community is stronger when it works together.
Twitter: @PeterJFoote1
Website: peterjfooteauthor.wordpress.com

Abandonment
by C.L. Williams

When you needed me, I was there with no hesitation. I came to your side at a time when you needed it most. In my time of need, you were absent. You even joked about abandoning me in my time of need. Now, we are at the place where I'm leaving you; the desert. I'm not going to kill you, I'll leave that to the sun, the snakes, whatever else is out there. You think it's funny to abandon me? Now I get the chance to laugh. I know one thing; I'll never have to deal with your absence again.

C.L. Williams is an international best-selling author currently living in central Virginia. He has written eight poetry books, four novellas, one novel, and a contributor to a multitude of anthologies and magazines. His most recent anthology appearance ANGELS: Dark Drabbles #2 from Black Hare Press became a number one in hot new releases. C.L. Williams is currently working on his second novel and a new poetry book.
Facebook: <u>writer434</u>
Twitter: <u>@writer_434</u>

Tech Era Revenge
by J.M. Meyer

The quiz I filled out yesterday made me sure Nathaniel was cheating.

1. Stopped wearing his wedding ring. "I've gained weight."

2. Sleeps with his phone. "For work emergencies."

3. Comes home late with vague excuses. "Norm's cat died."

Our love was dead. So, while he showered this morning, I read his texts, packed a suitcase and left him, forever.

I've a parting surprise of my own for Nathaniel. You see, I switched around his contacts' numbers. His saintly mom will receive the texts meant for Always Ready Amy. Messages for Bondage Bonnie will go to his boss. Sexy Sadie's…

J.M. Meyer is a writer, artist and small business owner living in New York, where she received her master's degree from Teachers College, Columbia University. Jacqueline enjoys writing speculative fiction and mysteries. Her favorite author is Alice Munro and her favorite film…is…anything horror related. Jacqueline also enjoys hiking with her dog Molly and the company of her husband Bruce and daughters; Julia, Emma and Lauren. Jacqueline's Mantra lately; there's no such thing as failing, it's called learning.
Website: jmoranmeyer.net
Amazon: www.amazon.com/author/jacquelinemoranmeyer

Remember Me
by Terri A. Arnold

I'm nobody. I'm tired of not being noticed. I haven't even been bullied throughout the years; in truth, I've simply been completely ignored. You could ask anyone I grew up with, I bet my life they would have no idea who you were talking about. It wouldn't even make them stop and think 'hmm, that name is familiar'. But I can promise you this, they'll know my name now, they'll never forget the name Dean Atwood. From this day forward I will stop being a nobody, I will be the topic of many discussions to come, everyone will remember me.

Terri A. Arnold is an avid reader turned writer from a small town in Nova Scotia, who has spent her life reading and wishing she was writing. Although she has written a lot in those years, she has only recently begun to submit pieces for publication. With ongoing encouragement from family and writing challenges with friends, Arnold felt the urge to try her hand at publishing.

Smiling
by Owen Morgan

She told me I needed to make more money. I smiled.

She insisted on expensive trips and grand expenditures for our anniversary, the best hotels, and food. I smiled.

Whenever something bad happened to her family, she insisted on dragging me into the conflict. She said you only live once, who needs to save money?

Now, at the end, I put my affairs in order. I have prepared my spouse for life without me. When I and all my money are gone, I will leave a note with my executor for her, which reads: I am still smiling, are you?

Owen Morgan *writes science fiction, fantasy, and alternate history, and lives in the fishing port of Steveston, British Columbia.*
Website: *httpwwwkingauthor.wordpress.com*
Twitter: *@owen_morgan1066*

Existing
by Dawn DeBraal

Herman hated getting up in the morning. He was thinking about quitting his job. If he quit, he would lose his apartment. If he lost the place, he would live out on the street. If he lived out on the street, he would have to eat from garbage cans and sleep under overpass bridges. If he slept outdoors, he'd get fleas, be cold and wet. Herman would still have to get up in the morning. He picked up the pistol, contemplating suicide. The only thing Herman hated worse than getting up in the morning was pain. So, he got up.

Dawn DeBraal lives in rural Wisconsin with her husband Red, two rat terriers, and a cat. She has discovered that her love of telling a good story can be written. Published stories with Palm-sized press, Spillwords, Mercurial Stories, Potato Soup Journal, Edify Fiction, Zimbell House Publishing, Clarendon House Publishing, Blood Song Books, Black Hare Press, Fantasia Divinity, Cafelit, Reanimated Writers, Guilty Pleasures, Unholy Trinity, The World of Myth, Dastaan World, Vamp Cat, Runcible Spoon, Dark Christmas, Siren's Call, Iron Horse Publishing, Falling Star Magazine 2019 Pushcart Nominee.
Amazon: amazon.com/Dawn-DeBraal/e/B07STL8DLX

Sins of the Father
by Maxine Churchman

The frail old man with pain wracked features was just moments from death. She used to call him Dad; he'd seemed so big and strong back then. It took months to track him down after her mother died, a small clue in some old documents giving impetus to her search.

He'd left them when her body matured, no longer to his taste. She'd found him just in time, before cancer took him.

Old hurts that had festered raised her ire again, and she twisted the knife in his belly once more. His suffering lasted deliciously longer than she'd dared hope.

Maxine Churchman lives in Essex UK and has recently started writing poetry and short stories to share. Her interests include learning to improve her writing, reading, knitting, walking and teaching yoga. She is also planning a novel.

Modern Hate
by David Bowmore

Do you know what I hate?

No? Then I'll tell you.

Modern films with impossibly attractive lead roles with perfect teeth and hair.

I hate modern cinemas too; buying tickets online and popcorn that rips my gums.

Footballers, who earn more in a week than I will in a lifetime.

And animal lovers who care more about cats than their own grandmothers.

And eco-activists—let's all go back to living in mud huts then. Wankers!

Young people, wearing next to nothing, going to festivals or climbing mountains and gurning into cameras. You didn't invent it, arseholes.

And I hate 'drink-a-fucking-ware.'

David Bowmore has lived here, there and everywhere, but now lives in Yorkshire with his wonderful wife and a small white poodle. He has worn many hats in his time; head chef, teacher and landscape gardener. His first collection of short stories 'The Magic of Deben Market' is available from Clarendon House.
Website: davidbowmore.co.uk
Facebook: davidbowmoreauthor

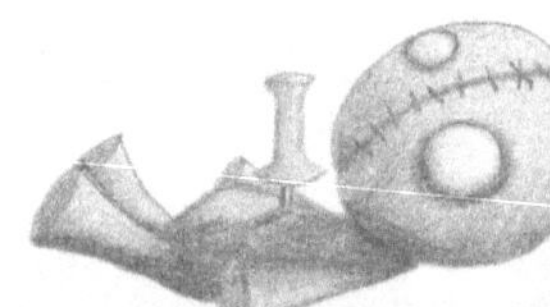

Noise Nuisance
by Jacek Wilkos

Tim listened to the noise that woke him. It was definitely a washing machine.

It was after midnight. The neighbour above was very problematic when it came to quiet hours.

I'll kill her, Tim thought, leaving the apartment.

He came back bloodstained and smiling. She won't bother him again. Ever. He left her body in the bathroom – on the floor, in the bathtub, some pieces even on the walls.

Tim took off his pyjamas, tossed into a laundry basin and soaked in warm water.

I'll wash it tomorrow, he thought, *I won't turn on the washing machine at this hour.*

Jacek Wilkos is an engineer from Poland. He lives with his wife and daughter in the beautiful city of Cracow. He is addicted to buying books, he loves coffee, dark ambient music and riding his bike. His work was published in Drablr, Rune Bear, Sirens Call eZine.
Facebook: Jacek.W.Wilkos

Nightmares
by K.T. Tate

I hate you. They said to let it go, that you were just a feeble old man, but I couldn't. The nightmare of crocodile smiles, corrupting hands and panting breath ever present. So, I studied. Not law but lore, forbidden and dangerous.

Now I watch as your face cracks with agony. As your skin blisters in eldritch patterns. It's simple really, I found your teeth and sold your soul. They're coming for you. Not demons, worse. Things that have tainted me to call, but nothing compares with the stain you left.

You took my childhood, now I'll take your eternity.

K.T. Tate lives in Cambridgeshire in the UK. She writes mainly weird fiction, cosmic horror and strange monster stories. Website: www.eldritch-hollow.com

Heartbeat
by David M. Donachie

A sane world wouldn't harvest the body of a victim to save the life of the driver, but seriously, I don't mind. When they put him on the operating table, his heart stopped, but mine was still beating even though I was dead. What were the doctors to do?

Now my heart beats in his chest. My blood rushes in his veins. Every day, he will hear the life he took thudding in his head. At night, I'll scream my name in his dreams. What's he going to do? Die? It's an excellent sort of revenge, I hope you'll agree.

David M. Donachie is an artist, author, and games designer. He has written short stories of countless types since he was old enough to hold a pencil — many are very embarrassing, the others appear in his self-published anthology The Night Alphabet, and in numerous anthologies. He lives in a garret (really a top-floor flat, but a garret sounds a lot more romantic) in Edinburgh with his wife Victoria, two cats, more reptiles than mammals, and more invertebrates than either.

Daydreams
by G. Allen Wilbanks

Bart walked slowly, stealthily through the house. The pistol felt cool and solid in his hand. Tiptoeing into the living room, he saw the back of Linda's head over the couch as she watched her daytime soap operas.

He raised the gun, levelled the sights on his wife's head, and pulled the trigger. The explosion of the weapon was loud and satisfying.

"Hey, stupid," shouted Linda, rousing Bart from his pleasant reverie. "What the hell are you smiling about? You imagining your dick is bigger than your thumb?"

"Was I smiling?" asked Bart, the gunshot still echoing in his mind.

G. Allen Wilbanks is a member of the Horror Writers Association (HWA) and has published over 100 short stories in various magazines and on-line venues. He is the author of two short story collections, and the novel, When Darkness Comes. Website: www.gallenwilbanks.com Blog: DeepDarkThoughts.com

Akazawa A'avik's Revenge
by Vonnie Winslow Crist

Haunted by her husband Hanzan's murder, Akazawa A'avik journeyed across the galaxy in a near light-speed vessel. She'd plotted revenge for years. Now that their younglings were adults, she'd repay the species which had shot down Hanzan's observation shuttle over the North American desert.

Hanzan had done no harm. Still, Earthlings had slaughtered her beloved.

When her ship sliced into Earth's atmosphere, Akazawa turned on a pre-recorded soundtrack. With crashing cymbals and hymns of jubilation ringing in her auditory receptors, Akazawa delivered cylinders of flesh-eating bacteria to the planet's seas.

Humans should be more careful who they offend, she mused.

Vonnie Winslow Crist is author of The Enchanted Dagger, Owl Light, The Greener Forest, Murder on Marawa Prime, and other award-winning books. Her fiction is included in "Amazing Stories," "Cast of Wonders," "Outposts of Beyond," Killing It Softly 2, Defending the Future - Dogs of War, Midnight Masquerade, Chaos of Hard Clay, and elsewhere. A cloverhand who has found so many four-leafed clovers she keeps them in jars, Vonnie strives to celebrate the power of myth in her writing.
Website: www.vonniewinslowcrist.com

Fresh Herbs
by Eddie D. Moore

Jason tripped over his muddy boots and nearly dropped the steaks. His ex-wife gasped and then chuckled.

"You still leave your shoes lying in everyone's way. I'm glad you didn't drop the food."

"This is my way of saying that we can be friends."

"I think so too. I'm sorry our breakup got ugly, but everyone exaggerates to gain the upper-hand." Jason placed a bottle on the table. "How special, you even remembered my fifty-seven sauce."

Jason smiled as his ex covered her food with the sauce and mumbled, "But it's the herbs I picked that make this meal *special*."

Eddie D. Moore travels hundreds of hours a year, and he fills that time by listening to audiobooks. When he isn't playing with his grandchildren, he writes his own stories. You can find a list of his publications on his blog or by visiting his Amazon Author Page. While you're there, be sure to pick up a copy of his mini-anthology Misfits & Oddities.
Website: eddiedmoore.wordpress.com
Amazon: amazon.com/author/eddiedmoore

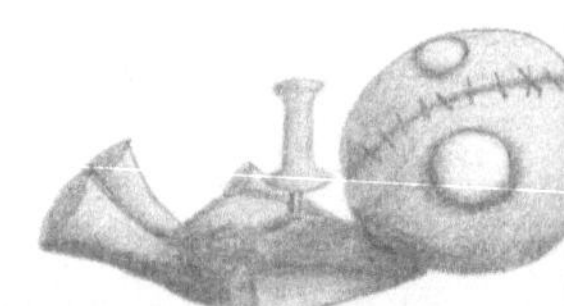

Stayin' Alive
by Shelly Jarvis

My girlfriend went out last night and didn't tell me. At the bar, shitfaced, sexy as hell. I didn't know until this morning when she wasn't home. I keep wondering whose bed she slept in.

I think about her all day, seething as my mind conjures images to spiral through my head. At home, I'm so worried about my girlfriend, I can barely acknowledge my wife.

I send Sarah a quick text while I take a bite of burger. Her phone's ringtone, Stayin' Alive, plays in my wife's apron.

"Oops," Amy says. "You were supposed to finish eating her first."

__Shelly Jarvis__ is a speculative fiction author from West Virginia, US. She found a life-long love of sci-fi and fantasy in the 3rd grade when she found Madeleine L'Engle's "A Wrinkle in Time." Shelly is an avid reader, a Whovian, the ideal viewer of dog rescue videos, and undoubtedly Ravenclaw. She currently has three YA sci-fi books available for purchase on Amazon. Website: www.ShellyJarvis.com

The Long Con
by N.M. Brown

We celebrate our ninth wedding anniversary this week. I'm thankful he married me even though we'll never have children.

He doesn't remember me from before, but I remember. I remember the red glare of his taillights after he realised he'd hit something. I remember screaming into the night air as my sister bled out into the street. And I remember the cigarette butt he tossed out the window as he drove away and left her there. The puddle of mud it landed in ruining all chance of DNA evidence.

I inject five of his veins with concentrated nicotine. Happy anniversary!

*Since **N.M. Brown** made her first post to a popular Internet forum, she's taken the horror community by storm. Her ability to create, terrify, and drive home her stories is insurmountable. N.M. Brown's published works can be found in multiple anthologies for all to read, but be forewarned, if you do... you may want to call your therapist after, her stories are terrifying, disturbing and devilishly unsettling. She is not only a fright visually, but also has a creepy tentacle in horror podcasting as well. Sinister Sweetheart writes, voice acts and is the media director of the Scarecrow Tales podcast.*
Website: Sinistersweetheart.wixsite.com/sinistersweetheart
Facebook: NMBrownStories

Bluebeard's Bloody Test
by McKenzie Richardson

My new husband's blue-toned beard crinkles in a grin as he entrusts me with the keys and shows me the door that I must never open. There is a malicious gleam in his eye, a playful sort of evil like an unspoken dare, a challenge, an invitation.

He places a scratchy kiss on my forehead before departing. I recall tales of the string of previous wives, their disappearances, how this castle reeks of blood. He thinks I will fail his test. But it will not be my blood spilt in this castle upon his return. I will avenge my predecessors.

McKenzie Richardson lives in Milwaukee, WI. Her horror stories have been featured in various anthologies including Evil Lurks, Pandemic, and After: Undead Wars. She has also published a variety of poems and flash fiction pieces.
Facebook: mckenzielrichardson
Blog: www.craft-cycle.com

The Hate You Make
by Liam Hogan

I find the witch pouring away a cauldron of noxious green slime.

"What's that?" I ask.

She pauses. "Hate potion, I guess."

"Hate potion?"

"When I make my love potions, I separate the hate from the love. But no-one wants hate potions, so..."

I think about my contacts—in America, in Europe, in the Middle East. Politicians, mainly, always on the search for new ways to control the masses.

I whip out my chequebook. "I'll take all the hate you make."

She looks at me wide-eyed. "What for?"

"Oh," I say, casual as I can. "I might have a buyer."

Liam Hogan is a London based short story writer, the host of Liars' League, and a Ministry of Stories mentor. His story "Ana", appears in Best of British Science Fiction 2016 (NewCon Press) and his twisted fantasy collection, "Happy Ending Not Guaranteed", is published by Arachne Press. Website: happyendingnotguaranteed.blogspot.co.uk Twitter: @LiamJHogan

Laughter
by Rhiannon Bird

She was laughing at me again; she would look at me then giggle with the other girls. The pencil was already in my hand, the scissors shaving off layers of wood.

My knuckles whitened around it. I couldn't hear anyone else, just her laughter echoing in my ears.

When the bell rang, I was out of my seat and sprinting through the woods behind school. I stopped when I reached the corner of Mason street. There I waited for her, then I could finally stop the laughing. Her voice floated towards me, and my grip on the sharped pencil tightened.

Rhiannon Bird is a young aspiring author. She has a passion for words and storytelling. Rhiannon has her own quotes blog; Thoughts of a Writer. She has had 4 works published. This includes 3 short stories and 2 poems. These are published on Eskimo pie, Literary yard, Down in the Dirt Magazine and Short break fiction. She can be found on Facebook, Instagram, and Pinterest.

Inconvenient
by Chris Bannor

They thought they were punishing him, sending him to the mining prison that circled Earth. They called him an eco-terrorist, but he was just a soldier in a war that humanity refused to take notice of. It was too inconvenient for them.

Too inconvenient to stop filling the oceans with plastic.

Too inconvenient to stop filling the skies with pollution.

Too inconvenient to stop filling the land with their population.

He wasn't alone though. Soon, they would act and humanity would see. The only humans left would be those off-planet. They would never return to inconvenience their Mother ever again.

Chris Bannor is a science fiction and fantasy writer who lives in Southern California. Chris learned her love of genre stories from her mother at an early age and has never veered far from that path. She also enjoys musical theater and road trips with her family but is a general homebody otherwise.
Facebook: chrisbannorauthor
Website: ChrisBannor.com

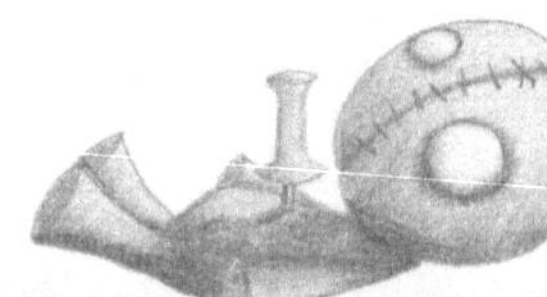

Reflected in her Eyes
by J.W. Garrett

Slipping through the mirror, Molly transitioned from one world into the next, seeking her stepmother. Reposed in sleep, calm rested across her face, belying her true nature. Night after night Molly endured physical and mental abuse under this woman's care.

"I've come for you."

Her stepmother's eyes snapped open, disbelief pooling in her gaze. "How?" she muttered. "You're a nightmare."

Waving hands through the air, Molly set items in motion. The bed skidded across the floor; curtains danced; clothing paraded around the room.

"It's time. Meet your fate."

Fear glazed her eyes.

Molly plunged inside the woman, stilling her heart.

J.W. Garrett has been writing in one form or another since she was a teenager. She currently lives in Florida with her family but loves the mountains of Virginia where she was born. Her writings include YA fantasy as well as short stories. Since completing Remeon's Quest-Earth Year 1930, the prequel in her YA fantasy series, Realms of Chaos, she has been hard at work on the next in the series, scheduled to release August 2020. When she's not hanging out with her characters, her favourite activities are reading, running and spending time with family.

Website: www.jwgarrett.com
BHC Press: www.bhcpress.com/Author_JW_Garrett.html

Serial Student
by Terri A. Arnold

I step carefully around the crime scene, taking in all the details. The amount of hatred needed to do something like this, it's unprecedented. I must find the person responsible. I can't let this happen again.

At least I can't let this happen again without the perp guiding me. This life—ending lives, ripping bodies to shreds—this is the life for me. Oh, the people I will end.

I notice a piece of hair, casually pick it up and place it in my pocket. This is the way; forensics. I will become his student, I will excel at murder.

Terri A. Arnold is an avid reader turned writer from a small town in Nova Scotia, who has spent her life reading and wishing she was writing. Although she has written a lot in those years, she has only recently begun to submit pieces for publication. With ongoing encouragement from family and writing challenges with friends, Arnold felt the urge to try her hand at publishing.

Hag
by Terry Miller

There were voices in Lisa's head. One was her own as a little girl, a little mischievous child that refused to grow up. Another was that of her angsty teenage youth. Then there was another voice, old, shaky, and coarse.

"You stupid whore! Take another drink, why don't you?" It would scream. So Lisa would drink; another and another.

Her days passed, intoxicated and lonely. One sober morning, she stood to stare at the reflected eyes of a tired, old woman.

With rage, her lips quivered. In a young voice, like that in her thirties, she bellowed, "You stupid hag!"

Terry Miller lives in Portsmouth, Ohio. His work has been featured in Sanitarium Magazine, Devolution Z, Jitter, Rhysling Anthology 2017, Poetry Quarterly, Sirens Call Ezine, The Horror Tree's Trembling With Fear, SpillWords, Organic Ink Vol. I, Curses & Cauldrons Anthology from Blood Song Books, Forest of Fear from Blood Song Books, the Dark Drabble Anthology Series from Black Hare Press, 100 Word Zombie Bites from Reanimated Writers Press, Scary Snippets, Guilty Pleasures & Other Dark Delights, 100 Word Horrors 3, and O Unholy Night In Deathlehem from Grinning Skull Press.
Facebook: tmiller2015
Amazon: amazon.com/author/millerterryl

A Soldier's Revenge
by Zoey Xolton

Xavier crept in the unlocked back door and into his fiancé's home. He climbed the old wooden staircase to the second story with practised stealth. He found her there, in bed, mid-coitus, with the male model she was cheating on him with.

He was fighting dissidents in foreign countries and she couldn't keep her legs together. Allowing his hate to grow, he leapt from the shadows and smashed the back of the sod's head in with a baseball bat. His skull slammed into Bethany's face, breaking her nose.

"Xavier, you psycho!" she screamed.

"Oh, baby girl. *You have no idea.*"

Zoey Xolton is an Australian Speculative Fiction writer, primarily of Dark Fantasy, Paranormal Romance and Horror. She is also a proud mother of two and is married to her soul mate. Outside of her family, writing is her greatest passion. She is especially fond of short fiction and is working on releasing her own themed collections in future.
Website: www.zoeyxolton.com

Ghost
by Cassandra Angler

You had warmed my side of the bed before my body had even gone cold.

You can't see me, but I'm here. Watching.

She looks happy to be there with you. Triumphant. I watch you do with her what you so often refused to do with me, my anger building.

Though my heart stopped beating, it's shattered.

I wait for your energy to fade, for sleep to come. I have eternity, after all—nothing left but patience. Her slow and steady breathing turns to panic as my icy hands tighten, clamped around her throat.

Cassandra Angler is a married mother of four who lives in the State of Ohio in the USA. When she isn't busy caring for her family, Cassandra works on her upcoming novel due out in November of 2020 titled Contaminated. Cassandra has three short story publications as well as several flash fiction and drabble publications.

I Am Sin
by Terry Miller

"Hatred is a sin!" the girl with the make-believe halo retorted, her face scrunched up like the devil himself.

Poppy snickered but kept her composure.

"I am sin!" Poppy replied.

The girl looked appalled by the remark.

Poppy looked her arrogant judge up and down, from the top of her bun to the bottom of her jean skirt.

"What do you think hell is really like?" she playfully inquired.

The girl just stared. Poppy approached her, doused her in whiskey from her flask, struck a match and flung it at her feet.

"Do you suppose it's a bit like that?"

Terry Miller lives in Portsmouth, Ohio. His work has been featured in Sanitarium Magazine, Devolution Z, Jitter, Rhysling Anthology 2017, Poetry Quarterly, Sirens Call Ezine, The Horror Tree's Trembling With Fear, SpillWords, Organic Ink Vol. I, Curses & Cauldrons Anthology from Blood Song Books, Forest of Fear from Blood Song Books, the Dark Drabble Anthology Series from Black Hare Press, 100 Word Zombie Bites from Reanimated Writers Press, Scary Snippets, Guilty Pleasures & Other Dark Delights, 100 Word Horrors 3, and O Unholy Night In Deathlehem from Grinning Skull Press. Facebook: tmiller2015
Amazon: amazon.com/author/millerterryl

Deconstructive Criticism
by Joanna Marsh

She was one of those people you couldn't help but hate. Who knew why?

Maybe her smile. Lips too thin, like a fish. Disgusting. It was practically a favour to cut those lips off.

Or that limp hair? Shear it off. Take the scalp, too.

Nose too big? Slam it into a wall. Watch the blood and bone drip out.

No. It had to be her eyes. Her cow-like eyes: dull and staring at her. So, she stabbed those eyes out too.

There. So much better.

How impressed the police would be when they found her.

"Worst suicide I've seen!"

Joanna Marsh is a Canadian fiction writer. Her works include 'Immortal Longings' in Aphrodite IX: Ares, 'Buffer' for the Prism Award-nominated comic anthology Group Chat by POMEgranate Magazine, and 'Bug Hunt' for the fiction anthology Nothing Without Us by Renaissance Press.
Twitter: @thriftbirds
Website: joannamarsh0.wixsite.com/mysite

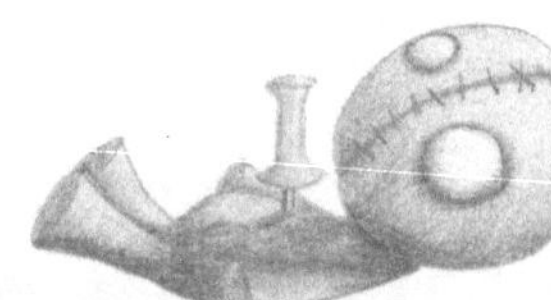

One More Slash
by Clint Foster

One more slash.

"I hate you."

One more slash.

"Do you remember all the times you let me down? All the times you deceived me, hurt me, got in my way?"

One more slash.

"I remember how you made me feel, how you treated me when I tried to give you the best. I remember the way you felt all these years."

One more slash.

"I could never forgive you for all that you've done, and I would never want to. I hate you. I always hated you, and always will. I hate you."

One last slash.

"I hate me."

Clint Foster lives with his herd of four cats, beloved Basset, Zero, and wonderful wife, Nik. He loves to tell stories just as much as he loves to read them, and is excited to share his work. A longtime consumer of media of all kinds, he enjoys giving back what he hopes everyone else thinks are good stories. Facebook: *ClintFosterAuthor*

Burning Bridges
by Annie Percik

Yet again, they didn't listen. I warned them, but nobody ever pays attention to me. And now the project is in the papers, with my name listed as the one responsible. There's talk of fines and maybe even prison time, and I'm the one slated to take the fall. Those corrupt bastards will just take their money and disappear off into the shadows. But not this time. Might as well be hung for a sheep as a lamb, as the old saying goes. I watch the last few drops of petrol soak into the office carpet and light the match.

Annie Percik lives in London with her husband, Dave, where she is revising her first novel whilst working as a University Complaints Officer. She writes a blog about writing and posts short fiction on her website, which is also where all her current publications are listed. She also publishes a photo-story blog, recording the adventures of her teddy—he is much more popular online than she is. She likes to run away from zombies in her spare time.
Website: www.alobear.co.uk
Blog: aloysius-bear.dreamwidth.org/

Current Mood
by Andrew Anderson

My twin sister Evelyn and I inherited the family mood rings, which had been in our family for three generations. The rings were colourless, but they would turn orange when in the presence of anyone who had ever endangered its owner.

My world collapsed when Evelyn was killed in a hit-and-run as she did her Christmas shopping—she was 23.

I wear her ring, and I've clocked up thousands of miles as I've hunted down her killer.

Four years I've searched, and today's the day.

I clench my fist, now glowing with a furious fire, and knock on the door.

Andrew Anderson is a spare-time writer of microfiction, flash fiction and short stories, from Bathgate, Scotland. His work has been published on FlashFlood and Re:Written, and published in Black Hare Press anthologies.
Twitter: soorploom

Trail
by Robin Braid

John kept pace as we raced through the woods. "Thanks for this."

"We were good friends, I miss that," I said.

"Amy shouldn't come between us," said John. "Just wasn't meant to be for you guys."

We ran deeper, side by side. I knew where to go. Climbing a long incline, over my shoulder I saw the town disappear below.

A cliff edge rose up ahead. I sprinted to it. "Easy there," said John.

"Do you think she'll blame you? I do," I said.

My gaze was fixed on John's face. I stepped backwards and let the world fall away.

Robin Braid writes stories of the mysterious and macabre. A resident of Fife, Scotland, he graduated from Dundee University with a degree in English Literature. When not working in his regular job he can often be found rambling over hills and glens in search of inspiration for further tales. Twitter: @robinbraid

A Sister's Love
by S.N. Graves

I scrubbed the caked-on blood from my fingers with my sister's pink toothbrush. The lavender soap helped break up the clots that formed around the matted hair tangled in my engagement ring, but it would likely do little for the deep, ruddy stains in the rug, or to dislodge the fragments of crusting skull and grey matter I'd ground into the fireplace's stonework in my frenzied crushing of her smug face. I'd slammed the hammer into her surgically perfect features until nothing remained but a pulpy, cherry-hued pudding in the centre... Her bare-toothed, lipless grin didn't look so smug now.

S.N. Graves was born in the South and can't see calling anyplace without a Waffle House home. She earned her M.F.A. in Popular Fiction from Seton Hill University in 2014 and was a senior editor at Loose Id LLC. She is twenty-three years happily married to the self-proclaimed victim of Stockholm syndrome, Brian David Graves, and enjoys duct taping her two adult sons to a chair and forcing them to read all the ugly first drafts of her books. Graves also freelance edits and creates art, including book covers.
Website: www.sngraves.com
Facebook: Shannon.N.Graves

Boredom and Change
by Radar DeBoard

Demetrisious hated boredom and ignorance, above everything else. Nothing else came close to making his blood boil as those two things.

Demetrisious always wanted to have things changing. Yet, he also didn't want people to become so use to change that they take it for granted, and then take for granted the person who made change possible.

For years, the human race had reached Demetrisious quota of ignorance, but it was today that he finally was bored enough to do something about it. As he rained fire upon the earth he laughed to himself, "This is going to be fun!"

Radar DeBoard is a horror movie and novel enthusiast who resides in the small town of Goddard, Kansas. He occasionally dabbles in writing, and enjoys to make dark tales for people to enjoy. He has had drabbles and short stories published in various electronic magazines and anthologies.
Facebook: WriterRadarDeBoard

Repeat the Question
by Nikki DeKeuster

"Why the obsession with me, Detective Weis?"

"Obsession? You're a file on my desk." Handcuffs ate into his wrists.

"How disappointing. Show some passion for your work." The knife skirted Weis's neck. "I do."

Weis braced for death. Something worse crackled in his ear. "Daddy?! Hel—" Two small voices trailed into gargling screams.

Straining against the metal chair, Weis growled. "You're dead!"

"You've discovered a better answer to my original question." The psychopath snickered. "Gotta run. If we don't see you in the next month, I'll mail the girls home to you in pieces. Dried, of course. Postage is expensive."

Nikki DeKeuster devours souls. She spits them onto her glowing screen and toys with their lives for your amusement. Reading this story makes you an accomplice to their suffering. You're welcome. A storyteller with decades of experience crafting tales with her friends, she's bound some of them to bring into the wider world. The stories, not her friends. She enjoys throwing stones into Lake Michigan with her daughter and keeping her husband up past his bedtime with her ramblings. The first novel in her horror series will claw its way out of the earth in 2020.
Website: NJDeKeuster.com

Time to Put on Those Dancing Shoes

by Jason Holden

The notice in the local paper was a sad one. An obituary of a mother taken early from her family. A tragic accident, so they think.

It didn't make me sad.

Nobody knows it was me who hacked the traffic lights, changing it from red to green too early; it took me five years to learn to do it. While she made herself a little family, forgetting all about me and the hurt she caused.

Tonight, I'll go to her grave again. Ten years ago, I told her I'd dance on her grave. Time to put on my dancing shoes.

Jason Holden is a human. He lives here and there in the UK, always with his wife, daughter and fur baby. His primary goal is to raise his daughter to adulthood without any major damage. When he can, he writes. He thinks he does it well, but you can be the judge of that. He has been published in a few anthologies here and there, has been praised and put down for his writing. You can find and follow him on Facebook, although he asks you only follow him on Facebook and not through the streets. That's just creepy.
Facebook: Jason Holden-Author

Roasting Marshmallows
by C.L. Williams

I sit here and roast marshmallows over a fire I created to let out my frustrations. I normally would not eat marshmallows, but today I made an exception. Today, I managed to rid myself of the one who caused the most grief and pain in my life. I got rid of them and now I am sitting here, over an open fire, roasting marshmallows. I know I'm going to regret this decision in the morning, but for now, I don't care. I'd ask you about your feelings on this, but your body is in the fire that's roasting my marshmallows.

C.L. Williams is an international best-selling author currently living in central Virginia. He has written eight poetry books, four novellas, one novel, and a contributor to a multitude of anthologies and magazines. His most recent anthology appearance ANGELS: Dark Drabbles #2 from Black Hare Press became a number one in hot new releases. C.L. Williams is currently working on his second novel and a new poetry book. Facebook: writer434
Twitter: @writer_434

Silence
by James Lipson

"Did you have a chance to read my story?"

Crickets.

"Hey there, sorry to bother you again. But have you had any time to read my short story?"

Nothing.

"Don't forget, I sent you a story to read!"

Silence.

It's not the criticisms that never come, nor the cadence of your uninterested wandering eyes. It's not the mention of the new book you started reading, or the ease in which you forget week after painful week, regardless of the self-demoralising reminders I force myself to send.

No, none of these hold a candle to the echoing stillness of your response.

James Lipson's debut book, Fallen and Other Stories, was published in 2019. His short stories have appeared in Black Hare Press Anthologies, Teleport Magazine, Inner Circle's Writers Group Anthologies, and others. With a background in art, James has naturally turned to illustrating as he writes, bringing many of his short stories to life not only with descriptive detail, but also detailed visual imagery.
Website: www.jameslipson.com
Instagram: jameslipsonart

The Fool
by Jennifer Hatfield

The first time John unzipped his jeans, Victoria fell in love. She hated him because she loved him. When she got pregnant, he demanded that she abort.

She stopped at his work site on her way home one day. The way his hands caressed her body was like a pianist playing Beethoven. She had an orgasm, from fantasizing about what was next.

John, pursuing his own orgasm, was pummelled in the head. Victoria dragged his body to the chipper, and flipped him in.

Horrendous sounds and blood curdling screams echoed through the woods.

A life was exchanged for a life.

Jennifer Hatfield spent a large portion of her life being a dedicated mother and wife. She managed her epilepsy diagnosis, and handled the loss of her husband. Grateful to find comfort in the ability to write in an effort to express her feelings, thoughts, and struggles. She's published 5 poems.

Road Rage
by Shawn M. Klimek

Facing bumper to bumper traffic at the freeway onramp, Murial signalled in vain for several minutes. When a boob in a Buick glanced down at his cellphone just as a gap opened, she surged forward to interpose her bumper. Oblivious, the boob rolled forward until he heard a scrape. His face turned white and he cursed, then stepped out of the car so hastily that he forgot to engage the brakes. Seeing a gun in his hand as he rounded his hood, Muriel instinctively backed up. Released, the Buick lurched forward, running him down. Muriel pulled in behind it, laughing.

Shawn M. Klimek *is the middle child of seven creative siblings, a globetrotting, U.S. military spouse, an internationally best-selling short-story writer, award-winning poet, and butler to a Maltese. More than one hundred and fifty of his stories and poems have been published in digital magazines or anthologies, including BHP's Deep Space, Eerie Christmas and every book so far in the Dark Drabbles series.*
Website: jotinthedark.blogspot.com
Facebook: shawnmklimekauthor

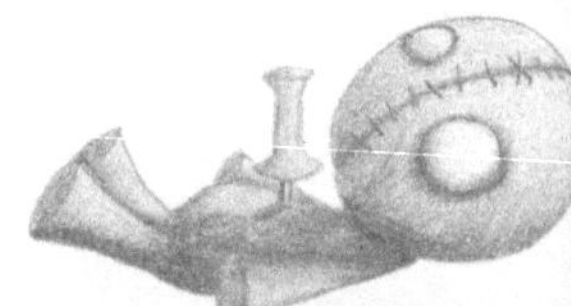

A New Horror Story
by Cindar Harrell

It's strange how easily love can turn to hate. I didn't believe it until I met her. She was the love of my life, and yet she will be the end of me, but I am determined to take her with me.

She moved on easily after leaving me to rot on the side of the road. I found her in the library and knew she would go to the back where the lights were dim.

I was there, waiting in the stacks of the horror section, knife at the ready.

It's time I gave her a new horror story.

Cindar Harrell loves fairy tales, especially ones with a dark twist. Her writing is often fairy tale inspired, but she also loves mystery and horror. Her stories can be found in various anthologies from publishers such as Black Hare Press, Iron Faerie Publishing, Dragon Soul Press, Blood Song Books, Soteira Press, Fantasia Divinity and more. Traveling is a passion for her as it inspires her imagination to run wild, especially in places that have a mystic presence in the air. She regularly moonlights as another human, but no matter who she is, she is always writing. Her novella inspired by The Snow Queen is set to release in 2020 as well as her debut novel, Lithium, and short story collection, Perchance to Dream. Facebook: CindarHarrell

Out of Time
by Dannielle Viera

It hadn't always been blue; in fact, until quite recently, his face had been crimson with rage. Reaching down, she tried to use her cuff to wipe away a trickle of dried blood from his temple. But the sanguine stain remained.

She had clocked him hard with his precious antique hourglass to stop his vicious attack, and now his time was up. Hers was just beginning. *A fitting end*, she thought. She stood and stretched, a feeling of freedom washing over her body. Stepping outside into the crisp winter air, she turned her pale face to the sun and smiled.

Dannielle Viera has been involved in the Australian publishing industry for over 20 years – first as a copywriter and then as an editor, project manager, proofreader and author. She has worked on over 100 non-fiction books, writing about subjects as varied as the history of Christianity, Native American mythology, vampires, knights and the death of Hollywood film stars. Some of the books for which she is credited as a contributor include Outside In Gains a Soul (ATB Publishing, 2019), A Christmas Cornucopia (Christmas Press, 2019), and Fire Burn, Cauldron Bubble: Magical Poems Chosen by Paul Cookson (Bloomsbury UK, 2020).
Facebook: DannielleVieraAuthor

Stupid People
by Stephen Herczeg

Everyday it's the same thing.

Those stupid people over the divider, talking their stupid talk about stupid subjects. Constant uninformed drivel of things they have no idea about.

I could have a better conversation with my shoe.

They make coffee with that stupidly loud machine of theirs, then stand around it for the next hour and talk absolute crap.

What's it today? Bad drivers? The Government? School kids? Who cares? Just shut up.

Hang on, it's working.

I put a little something extra in their machine this morning. They've all gone quiet, except for the dull thuds.

Peace at last.

Stephen Herczeg is an IT Geek based in Canberra Australia. He has been writing for over twenty years and has completed a couple of dodgy novels, sixteen feature length screenplays and numerous short stories and scripts. His horror work has featured in Sproutlings, Hells Bells, Below the Stairs, Trickster's Treats #1 and #2, Shades of Santa, Behind the Mask, Beyond the Infinite; The Body Horror Book, Anemone Enemy, Petrified Punks and Beginnings. He has also had numerous Sherlock Holmes stories published through the Belanger Books - Sherlock Holmes anthologies.
Amazon: amazon.com/-/e/B07916SQQS
Facebook: stephenherczegauthor

A Little Bit of Torture
by Jodi Jensen

She could kill him.

He deserved it.

But there were other ways, better ways to make him pay.

Rowan hummed softly as she gathered her carefully acquired corn husks, twine, sticks, and moss, then assembled the doll.

Finally, she turned to where he sat, gagged and bound to a chair, and snipped a large swath from his shirt.

After she'd dressed and baptised the doll, she turned to her ex-lover once again. His wide eyes, muffled pleas, and ineffectual struggles fuelled the darkness inside of her.

She picked up a pin and grinned. "Shall we begin today's lesson on cheating?"

Jodi Jensen, *author of time travel romances and speculative fiction short stories, grew up moving from California, to Massachusetts, and a few other places in between, before finally settling in Utah at the ripe old age of nine. The nomadic life fed her sense of adventure as a child and the wanderlust continues to this day. With a passion for old cemeteries, historical buildings and sweeping sagas of days gone by, it was only natural she'd dream of time traveling to all the places that sparked her imagination.*
Twitter: @WritesJodi
Facebook: jodijensenwrites

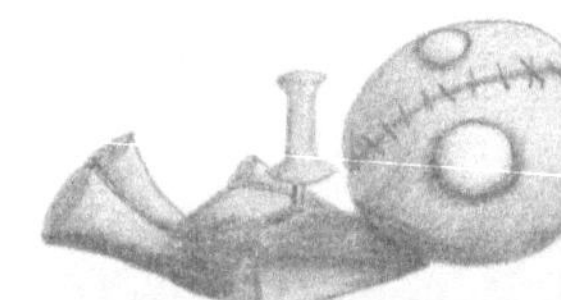

A Dance with Suspicion
by Carole de Monclin

I don't blame the siren. I blame the man.

Sirens tempt, but a good man should resist the call. Mine didn't.

Again, he pretends to work late.

I wait in the dark ruminating. Time swallowed my curves and lined my face. It gave him rugged charm.

The gravel crunches under his tyres and my grip tightens on the gun. He bought it for protection. My dignity and pride need protecting.

My finger doesn't hesitate. In the bitter silence that follows, I pry a card from his hand,

"Surprise. Three months of clandestine lessons, and I can tango now. Let's dance."

Carole de Monclin travels both the real world and imaginary ones. She's lived in France, Australia, and the USA; visited 25+ countries; and explored Mars, Ceres, and many distant planets. She writes to invite people on a journey. Her stories can be found in The Arcanist, The Deep Space Anthology, and every volume of the Dark Drabbles series.
Website: CaroledeMonclin.com
Twitter: @CaroledeMonclin

Jennifer's Lament
by Stuart Conover

Jennifer and Jonah were cursed to be.

From a deal he struck, they'd be married eternally.

A young man she'd once been nice to in passing

Had turned to stalking her and harassing.

Jennifer thought she'd gotten rid of him.

But now her future appeared to be grim.

Jonah made a pact with a demon in disguise.

Now she would be forced to look into his eyes.

And at the alter say "I Do"

Though Jennifer had planned a coup.

The last of the vows were "Till death do you part."

Immediately after, she'd plunge a dagger into his heart.

Stuart Conover is a father, husband, rescue dog owner, published author, blogger, journalist, horror enthusiast, comic book geek, science fiction junkie, and IT professional. With all of that to cram in daily, we have no idea if or when he sleeps or how he gets writing done! (We suspect it has to do with having evil clones.) Stuart is a Chicago native and runs the author resource Horror Tree.

The Guardian
by James Lipson

If he ever gets close enough, I swear I will bite him, you'll see! How many times must he fail before realising he'll never win? I am the guardian of my domain, an ever-vigilant hero standing patrol while those I have sworn to protect rest comfortably inside.

At noon today, like every day, I will meet my adversary at the border, I will look into his dead grey eyes and tell him, "Not Today!"

***

"Marcus, as soon as the mail gets here, please go get it. Oh, and don't let Haley out, you know how much she hates the mailman."

James Lipson's debut book, Fallen and Other Stories, was published in 2019. His short stories have appeared in Black Hare Press Anthologies, Teleport Magazine, Inner Circle's Writers Group Anthologies, and others. With a background in art, James has naturally turned to illustrating as he writes, bringing many of his short stories to life not only with descriptive detail, but also detailed visual imagery.
Website: www.jameslipson.com
Instagram: jameslipsonart

Cancer
by Ximena Escobar

Alice didn't recognise the healer. Dressed in rags, she looked too much like the awful woman in her mirror, so she turned her and her drops of 'Forgiveness' away. Instead, she fantasised about disfiguring Susan's face with acid.

But bitterness had already taken its toll and that same untameable hatred that would hurt Susan—stronger than her curses, louder than glass breaking—materialised into a murderous mass.

Like white flags rising, Alice finally let go.

Now she feels happy when birds perch by her window; smiles at the flowers by her deathbed…

Forgiveness heals… Don't let it in too late.

Ximena Escobar is writing stories and poetry. Originally from Chile, she is the author of a translation into Spanish of the Broadway Musical "The Wizard of Oz", and of an original adaptation of the same, "Navidad en Oz", both produced in her home country. Since 2018 she has published several short stories in various anthologies and online platforms, and is now slowly working on her own collection. Ximena has a degree in Arts & Communication Science and lives in Nottingham with her family.
Facebook: Ximenautora
Twitter: @laximenin

Al Moto's Revenge
by J.B. Wocoski

Tired of Souto, my most arrogant friend, betraying me again by stealing my latest girlfriend, I plotted my revenge.

On New Year's Eve, my plan came to fruition as I purposefully ran into him in a saki bar. I found him inebriated from already drinking heavily. Everyone egged me on as I toasted him, again and again, with impunity.

Later, as I led him away, they had no idea of what I was going to do beneath the docks of Tokyo. I chained and gagged this drunken sot and left him to drown in the high tide and to rot.

J.B. Wocoski is the author and narrator of the shortstorypodcast.com with three flash fiction short story books published in the last three years. He is currently working on book 4 "Short Story Podcast 2019." He writes mostly science fiction, fantasy, and horror stories. He won the 2016 Little Tokyo Short Story Writing Contest with his short story "The Last Master of Go"
Website: shortstorypodcast.com

Loathing
by C.L. Williams

"I hate you!" he said while staring down his nemesis.

"This will be the FINAL TIME you do something to ruin me!" he added.

He was angry at someone for being done wrong, his heart now filled with hate.

"I am going to get my revenge on you for everything you have EVER done to me. I'll see to it you never ruin anyone the way you ruined me!" He finished his rant and grabbed a knife.

It was at that moment when the revelation happened; he was yelling at the mirror. He walked away, and he slit his wrists.

C.L. Williams is an international best-selling author currently living in central Virginia. He has written eight poetry books, four novellas, one novel, and a contributor to a multitude of anthologies and magazines. His most recent anthology appearance ANGELS: Dark Drabbles #2 from Black Hare Press became a number one in hot new releases. C.L. Williams is currently working on his second novel and a new poetry book. Facebook: writer434 Twitter: @writer_434

Going Down, Sir?
by Andrew Anderson

Naomi burned with fury when she saw The Man spit upon Jake.

Jake was a friendly homeless man who occupied the top step of the longest vertical staircase in the city—281 steps. It was a prime spot, milling with wealthy tourists here for the world-famous arts festival.

Jake only begged until he had enough money for a bed for the night; Naomi empathised, having been homeless herself once.

Naomi lost count of how many stairs The Man hit on the way down when she pushed him. The applauding tourists thought it was a performance…until they saw the blood.

Andrew Anderson is a spare-time writer of microfiction, flash fiction and short stories, from Bathgate, Scotland. His work has been published on FlashFlood and Re:Written, and published in Black Hare Press anthologies.
Twitter: soorploom

The Last Dance
by Kimberly Rei

The fox glared through the hazy window. The witch inside took no notice, and that was fine. It was going to take the fox some time to gather his resources.

Never again would he walk on two legs. Never again would he dance with a girl or enjoy sweet wine. The witch had seen to that.

His yipping howls drew others of his kind. Those who remembered but could not revisit. Those she had doomed to a short burst of life.

Throughout the night, they gathered around the cabin. As the sun crested the horizon, they moved in as one.

Kimberly Rei has been writing for as long as she can remember. At five years old, her parents gifted her with a set of Children's Classics that she had no hope of reading. Yet. The potential alone sparked a love of words that has never wavered. Kim has taught writing workshops and edited novels for Authors You May Recognize. She has published several short stories and now can't stop chasing paper dragons. She currently lives in Tampa Bay, Florida with her wife and an abundance of gorgeous beaches to explore.

My Own Vengeance
by Brandi Hicks

The ketamine was working perfectly. I had him strapped to the chair just in case, but he wasn't moving a muscle. He could still feel everything, you could tell it in his eyes. Those same eyes that watched as the life drained out of my wife.

I took the next bamboo chute off the surgical tray and shoved it under his fingernail. Those grimy fingers that wrapped around her throat as he defiled her body. His eyes plead with me, but I will show no remorse. He will pay for everything he did; slowly, he will pay with his life.

*Growing up in West Virginia, **Brandi Hicks** loved to have her nose in a book, her eyes toward the night sky and putting a pen to paper. Her imagination was always sparked by her grandfather and her mom taking her to new places and teaching her about the unusual. She loves fantasy, sci-fi, and learning about science and history. She has two beautiful children, and hopes to instill creativity and a love of reading in them. Finding new crafts to try keeps her busy when not playing with her kids or working.*

Just Stop It
by Stuart Conover

Janet couldn't take it anymore.

"Please stop it," she asked the men who kept talking to her.

Suggesting things to her.

Rubbing up against her.

"Just stop it," she cried to the one who followed her into her home.

He didn't.

She refused to be broken.

Hurt, angry, lost, Janet cried out into the night.

She would do anything for revenge.

Surprisingly, something answered her.

The demon spoke in a language not her own.

Yet she knew what it asked.

The price she had to pay.

Accepting it, an ebony blade formed in her hand.

Now she could stop it.

Stuart Conover is a father, husband, rescue dog owner, published author, blogger, journalist, horror enthusiast, comic book geek, science fiction junkie, and IT professional. With all of that to cram in daily, we have no idea if or when he sleeps or how he gets writing done! (We suspect it has to do with having evil clones.) Stuart is a Chicago native and runs the author resource Horror Tree.

Bloody Revenge
by Emma K. Leadley

They called her the heartbreaker. With long dark hair, full red lips and a smile that lit up the valley, every man in the village lusted after her. No woman thought their husband safe. But it was ill-deserved a reputation; she only ever wanted one man. Alas, he was betrothed to another and turned her down time after time, his future wife becoming ever more enraged.

No-one did find out what happened that fateful night. Suicide? Murder? Now, wives lock up their husbands and mothers their sons, from dusk through till dawn. For the heartbreaker's revenge is bloody and literal.

Emma K. Leadley *is a UK-based writer, creative geek, and devourer of words, images and ideas. She began writing both fiction and creative non-fiction as an outlet for her busy brain, and quickly realised scrawling words on a page is wired into her DNA.*
Website: emmaleadley.co.uk
Twitter: @autoerraticism

The Case of the Tortured Torso
by John H. Dromey

"You're accused of carving your initials next to those of your new boyfriend while in a public park. You then outlined the initials with the shape of a heart. Correct?"

"Yes."

"I specialise in felony murder cases. Why do you need my services?"

"I made some of the cuts rather deep."

"Trees are resilient. Even if you penetrated the bark, you surely wouldn't have done permanent damage to the trunk. I think the magistrate will be inclined to show some leniency. Love is a powerful motive."

"So is hate. I carved the initials in the *trunk* of my old boyfriend."

John H. Dromey was born in northeast Missouri, USA. He enjoys reading—mysteries in particular—and writing in a variety of genres. In addition to contributing to the Black Hare Press series of Dark Drabbles anthologies, he's had short fiction published in Alfred Hitchcock's Mystery Magazine, Martian Magazine, Mystery Weekly, Stupefying Stories Showcase, Thriller Magazine, Unfit Magazine, and elsewhere, as well as in numerous anthologies, including Chilling Horror Short Stories (Flame Tree Publishing, 2015).

He Loves Me Not
by Zoey Xolton

Kataryna watches as the last petal falls, and her aching heart turns to ice. Snatching up her Book of Shadows, she stormed to her cauldron. She throws whole vials of precious, rare herbs in, not willing to take chances.

He will pay for breaking my heart!

Hissing words of power, she curses the count who professed his undying love, only to deflower her, and cast her aside.

Full of cold rage, she seals the spell with a lock of his golden hair, and her own crimson blood.

The count would bear no children, and history would not remember his name.

Zoey Xolton is an Australian Speculative Fiction writer, primarily of Dark Fantasy, Paranormal Romance and Horror. She is also a proud mother of two and is married to her soul mate. Outside of her family, writing is her greatest passion. She is especially fond of short fiction and is working on releasing her own themed collections in future.
Website: www.zoeyxolton.com

Over a Steak
by C.L. Williams

Stan and Lee took a walk on the pier, laughing about old times.

"Lee?" Stan asks, "Remember that time you ate my steak?"

Lee laughs, "That steak was delicious! You told me you were going to kill me for eating the most delicious steak ever cooked!"

"I'm sure it was," Stan says before pulling a gun on Lee, "Now I'm here to collect on my promise."

Lee, still thinking Stan is joking, continues laughing. That is, until Stan fires a shot at Lee's feet.

"You son of a—" Lee begins to say before Stan fires a shot in Lee's head.

C.L. Williams is an international best-selling author currently living in central Virginia. He has written eight poetry books, four novellas, one novel, and a contributor to a multitude of anthologies and magazines. His most recent anthology appearance ANGELS: Dark Drabbles #2 from Black Hare Press became a number one in hot new releases. C.L. Williams is currently working on his second novel and a new poetry book. Facebook: writer434
Twitter: @writer_434

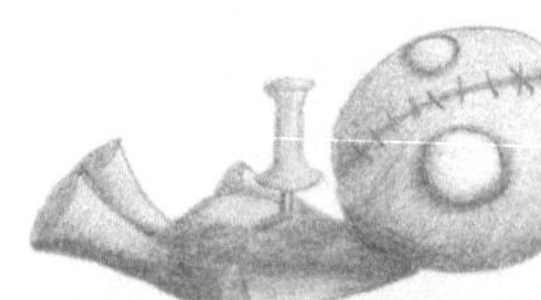

Blackmail
by Trisha Ridinger McKee

Dinah pasted on a bright smile. "How's the pot roast?"

"Delish," Norman answered. She tried not to visibly cringe.

She turned so the camera caught her grin. So Cheri could see from five states away how Dinah had stolen her life, her husband, her home.

She wanted Cheri to see that she had won after years of competing. By sheer luck of discovering Cheri's embezzlement at the bank they both worked at, Dinah had finally gotten the upper hand. She had control. She won.

She was stuck with a man she hated, but she had really stuck it to Cheri.

Trisha Ridinger McKee resides in a small town in Pennsylvania where love has proven to be a problem. Her work has appeared or is forthcoming in publications such as Tablet Magazine, The Oddville Press, Crab Fat Literary Magazine, Night to Dawn Magazine, Deep Fried Horror, 4 Star Stories, and more.

Waste Not, Want Not
by Dale Parnell

Farming is a busy life, even more so since Grandma passed. She liked to keep herself occupied, used to say that idleness was the devil's playground. She'd get so angry, spitting bile and railing against the layabouts and wastrels we'd see in town, nothing to do but count their fingers. I hear her voice at night, cussin' up a storm and telling me I have to do something about it.

I think I've finally done it, found a use for all those wasters letting their lives slip away.

That's the thing with pig farming, you always need more animal feed.

Dale Parnell *lives in Staffordshire, England, with his wife and their imaginary dog, Moriarty. He has self-published two collections of short stories, "The Green Cathedral" and "Bramble and other stories". Dale also writes poetry, and is lucky enough to have pieces featured in several poetry and fiction anthologies.*
Facebook: _shortfictionauthor_

The Ex
by Lyndsey Ellis-Holloway

My pulse was deafening, thumping rapidly within my ears, drowning out his gurgling, gasping breaths.

My hands ached, the pressure exerted by my fingers caused my arms to shake with the effort to keep my grip.

Tears flowed from my eyes; fixed upon his as he looked at me in desperation. I did not care. Not anymore.

I felt his flesh strain beneath my palms, his fingers clawing at mine as he tried to breathe.

Rage like I have never known filled me, consumed every part of me.

I watched the life leave his eyes.

He couldn't hurt me now.

Lyndsey Ellis-Holloway is a writer from Knaresborough, UK. She writes fantasy, sci-fi, horror and dystopian stories, focussing on compelling characters and layering in myth and legend at every opportunity. Her mind is somewhat dark and twisted, and she lives in perpetual hope of owning her own Dragon someday, but for now she writes about them to fill the void... and to stop her from murdering people who annoy her. When she's not writing she spends time with her husband, her dogs and her friends enjoying activities such as walking, movies, conventions and of course writing for fun as well! Website: theprose.com/LyndseyEH

Bitter Tea
by R.A. Goli

Tamsin clutched her belly as the last of the contractions hit. They were easing now; the red chunks and clots had ceased. Now, only blood spilled from her womanhood.

It was the moon-tea Madam Davene made all the courtesans drink. Now, Tamsin would never be able to bear children, even when she was ready to.

She stood, exhausted, and cleaned herself and the bedding. Then she prepared a different tea, especially for the madam, with a few special herbs purchased from a magi mixed in. She stirred the bitter liquid.

The drink would do a lot more than prevent children.

R.A. Goli is an Australian writer of horror, fantasy, and speculative short stories. In addition to writing, her interests include reading, gaming, the occasional walk, and annoying her dog, two cats, and husband. You can check out her numerous publications including her fantasy novella, The Eighth Dwarf, and her collection of short stories, Unfettered on her website and sign up to her newsletter for free short stories, updates and other fun stuff.
Website: ragoliauthor.wordpress.com/
Facebook: RAGoliAuthor

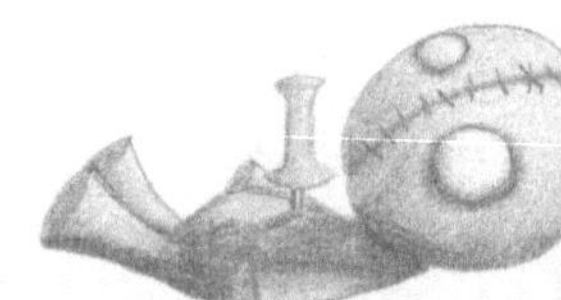

My Lover's Lover
by Shelly Jarvis

My lover's lips are stained in red,
They whisper out my name.
I lift her up onto the bed,
To finish out our game.

With paring knife, I slice her face,
With boning, rip her thighs.
I laugh at lover's quiet grace—
Poised, even as she cries.

My best friend's corpse is in the floor.
I barely felt a thing,
When I ripped out his bleeding heart
And put it with her ring.

Once I would've blanched at this,
To think that I would hurt her;
But then she turned from mine to his
And my heart turned to murder.

Shelly Jarvis is a speculative fiction author from West Virginia, US. She found a life-long love of sci-fi and fantasy in the 3rd grade when she found Madeleine L'Engle's "A Wrinkle in Time." Shelly is an avid reader, a Whovian, the ideal viewer of dog rescue videos, and undoubtedly Ravenclaw. She currently has three YA sci-fi books available for purchase on Amazon. Website: www.ShellyJarvis.com

Pre-existing Condition
by Raven Corinn Carluk

Tara's sobs woke him. Karl opened his eyes and fought a wave of nausea. His wife screamed, and his heart raced.

Strange hands clamped down on his shoulders. "Just in time."

"Who...are..." Karl's voice cracked, and he struggled against his bonds.

"Just one of your many nameless victims." The stranger crossed to Tara and checked her bonds. "Just another person who had to watch his wife suffer while jumping through every hoop your insurance company gave while her immune system ate her alive."

He met Karl's gaze with a rictus grin. "I won't let yours suffer nearly as long."

Raven Corinn Carluk writes dark fantasy, paranormal romance, and anything else that catches her interest. She's authored five novels, where she explores themes of love and acceptance. Her shorter pieces, usually from her darker side, can be found in Black Hare Press anthologies, at Detritus Online, and through Alban Lake Publishers.
Twitter: @ravencorinn
Website: www.ravencorinncarluk.com

Not Enough Coffee
by Zoey Xolton

The editor sat slumped in his chair, illuminated by the glow of his screen. He was so tired that it felt like his eyes were bleeding. There just wasn't enough coffee to lift his dour mood.

An alert, a new email. He sighed. Another impatient, self-important author pestering him for a response on their submission.

And these people call themselves professionals!

In his dreams, he'd burn them and their submissions, dancing around a great bonfire as their hopes, dreams and lives went up in smoke.

Smiling at the thought, he pushed the offending email to the back of the queue.

Zoey Xolton is an Australian Speculative Fiction writer, primarily of Dark Fantasy, Paranormal Romance and Horror. She is also a proud mother of two and is married to her soul mate. Outside of her family, writing is her greatest passion. She is especially fond of short fiction and is working on releasing her own themed collections in future.
Website: www.zoeyxolton.com

You Said You Wouldn't, But You Did
by Monica Schultz

"Lying, filthy, cheat!"

With each word Morgan hurtles another frame off the wall, watching it shatter against the hardwood. A million pieces. Her chest heaves, fighting the urge to scream.

"I did it for you," Hans insists without a hint of remorse. "Rage creates powerful witches."

Morgan's eyes narrow. Shards of glass and splintered wood lift from the floor, hovering mid-air.

"Perfect, now recreate the frame."

The air shimmers as the jagged fragments collect before Morgan, concealing the fury burning in her eyes. With a cruel smile she drives every sliver home, piercing the heart that betrayed the wrong woman.

Monica Schultz is a full-time Mathematics and History teacher from Ipswich, Australia, with a passion for writing fantasy. When she isn't busy finding 'x' in the latest equation, you can find her curled up with a young adult book and a cat on her lap. Website: https://monicaschultzauthor.weebly.com/ Instagram: @monicaschultzauthor

Monster
by T.W. Garland

They left the courtroom, faces pale and hands shaking.

"Is it possible?" she asked.

"Possible?" he said. "Did you hear the charges? The evidence? All those things. All those horrible things."

"Yes, but…"

"How can a person do that to another person, let alone his own sister? And so many times."

"You heard his lawyer; he didn't know what he was doing."

"He knows what he did. He's a monster. He enjoyed it. It's sickening."

"He deserves our love no matter what."

"Our love? Are you kidding? After everything he's done, how you can you say that?"

"He's our son."

T.W. Garland *has a stack of Victorian novels that taunt him with their unbroken spines. He has published stories containing monster hunters, supernatural creatures, steampunk adventurers, aberrations of nature, crazed criminals and psychic detectives. He buys more books than he could hope to read and is glad not to have been born in the nineteenth century or in a novel by Dickens. One day he hopes to live in the real world.*
Website: twgarland.wordpress.com

New Neighbours
by Kevin Berg

It started out pleasant enough.

Young couple with a dog and their ghost—some kid they lost at the last place they lived. Too violent, they'd said. So, they came here looking for a new start.

I hated that fucking dog.

A steak marinated in antifreeze shushed everything for a bit—until they got another puppy. Couple of friendly iced teas with some strychnine made sure they learned the lesson and only left me a couple of holes to dig.

To be honest, now I'm kind of fond of the puppy, though he keeps digging at the graves.

Stupid mutt.

Kevin Berg is the author of Indifference, Daddy Monster, and Ants in My Blood. His dark fiction can be found at Pulp Metal Magazine, Near to the Knuckle, The Blood Red Experiment, Horror Sleaze Trash, Trembling With Fear, Underbelly Magazine, Stupefying Stories, and Alien Buddha Press, among others. He currently resides in the Land of Smiles.

This Little Piggy
by A.R. Dean

Feet. I gag at the word. Worthless, disgusting appendages. I sit in my booth as the ignorant people flood by, unaware that they are walking on evil.

Summer is here; there's sandals and flip-flops everywhere. The epidemic of feet must come to an end. Each flash of the skinned hooves makes me rage.

I must wait for the dark to set them free. They have no idea how I will enrich their lives by hacking away those grotesque extremities. I did it to my own and can now admire my legs without vomiting at the sight of them.

Here piggies.

A.R. Dean is a dark and twisted soul. Dean has spent their whole life spreading fear with the tales from their head. Best known for stories that terrify and show the evilest side of human nature. So, look for Dean haunting your local cemetery or under your bed, because they're here to spread the fear. Turn off your lights and enjoy a scare. Dean is being published in Black Hare Press's Beyond and Unravel Anthologies. Keep a lookout for more stories.

Facebook: A.R. Dean Author & Ghoul

Leaving Gift
by Dale Parnell

"I'm sorry, Tim," she said, "but I just don't love you anymore."

I cried. She would have been suspicious if I didn't. I knew this was coming. There are always signs, if you look close enough.

A friend of a friend taught me the summoning spell. I'd drawn the runes last weekend, and I hid the blood when I was supposedly packing my things to leave.

Now all it needs is a full moon, there's one due in three days. And then they will come for her.

If I wait outside the house, maybe I can even hear the screams.

Dale Parnell lives in Staffordshire, England, with his wife and their imaginary dog, Moriarty. He has self-published two collections of short stories, "The Green Cathedral" and "Bramble and other stories". Dale also writes poetry, and is lucky enough to have pieces featured in several poetry and fiction anthologies.
Facebook: shortfictionauthor

Hate Runs in the Family
by T.A. Ulven

People would ask me if I hated my father for killing my mother. *Yes*, I'd say without flinching. But it was a lie. I didn't hate him for that. I hated him for the years of abuse, torture and humiliation. I hated him for existing.

Given the chance, would I kill him?

No. That would be too easy. I wanted him to suffer the rest of his life. Abused, tortured, humiliated. Locked up like the animal he is.

He didn't deserve to die. My mother did. That's why I killed her. That's why I framed him.

And now I'm free.

T.A. Ulven *is a father, husband, and horror fiction writer hailing from the cold mountains of Norway. He became known through his horror persona hyperobscure, primarily posting short stories on the vast writing subreddit of NoSleep. He has since had work published in several anthologies, and will continue to expand his dark universe for as long as people will visit it.*
Facebook: hyperobscure
Reddit: hyperobscura

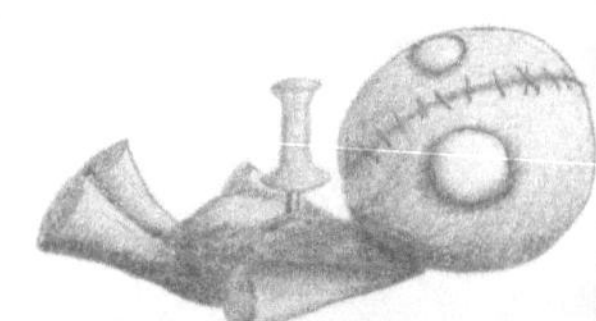

Just a Friend
by G. Allen Wilbanks

"I heard you went out with some other girl last night. Are you breaking up with me?" asked Darlene.

"It's not like that. She's just a friend," Carlton tried to assure his angry girlfriend.

"Really? Because I have friends, too. In fact, I called one of them this morning."

"Are you going out with him?"

"He's not that kind of friend," Darlene said, coldly.

"Well, what kind of friend is he?"

"He's the kind of friend you pay a large amount of money, then you don't hear from him again until he calls you to say the job is done."

G. Allen Wilbanks is a member of the Horror Writers Association (HWA) and has published over 100 short stories in various magazines and on-line venues. He is the author of two short story collections, and the novel, When Darkness Comes. Website: www.gallenwilbanks.com Blog: DeepDarkThoughts.com

Meet at 0600 Hours,
Top of the World Hotel
by Jacob Bowers

I woke up still tired from the flight. Slept well, though. The hotel had starchy bedding, like mine and Michelle's old sheets.

They told him to meet on top of the hotel. Wear civvies. There, he'd get his next mission. Someone would be there to rendezvous.

He took it: hook, line, and sinker.

I wore the dark suit. The handgun was in the shoulder holster.

"A sniper would be easier," they said, "Put you near the top—"

"No." I wanted to hear the little gasp.

No mercy now. This one's for Michelle.

I clicked the "up" button on the elevator.

Jacob Bowers is a student at Franciscan University of Steubenville, majoring in English. He enjoys reading, writing fiction, watching any kind of movie, and debating obscure theological topics.

Prayer
by Dale Parnell

They called it a hate crime. Damn right it was. Thirty-one years of devout faith, going to church twice a week. And for what? For You to randomly decide You're going to take my husband and child from me.

A freak accident, they said. Couldn't have been prevented, they said. God's mysterious plan, they said. What possible plan requires a six-week-old baby?

So yes, I burned down eight of your churches before they finally caught me. Burned them right down to the ground.

They tell me there's a chapel in the prison.

Good.

Because I'm not nearly finished hating You.

Dale Parnell lives in Staffordshire, England, with his wife and their imaginary dog, Moriarty. He has self-published two collections of short stories, "The Green Cathedral" and "Bramble and other stories". Dale also writes poetry, and is lucky enough to have pieces featured in several poetry and fiction anthologies.
Facebook: shortfictionauthor

Fury
by Gabriella Balcom

Obsessing about his ex-wife Viola's upcoming marriage, Lemuel remembered her infidelity and fumed. He merged with the wind and sent gales swirling in all directions.

Rage and hatred intensifying as he swept across town, he blasted open Viola's door, finding her in her beau's arms. Lemuel raked them with jagged talons of air, ripped them to pieces, and didn't stop till they lay shredded on the floor.

Unsatisfied, he gusted one direction, then another, pulverized everything in his path, and ignored the blood flying through the air. He didn't stop until he'd levelled the city and body parts lay everywhere.

Gabriella Balcom lives in Texas with her family, loves reading and writing, and thinks she was born with a book in her hands. She works in a mental health field, and writes fantasy, horror/thriller, romance, children's stories, and sci-fi. She likes travelling, music, good shows, photography, history, interesting tales, and animals. Gabriella says she's a sucker for a great story and loves forests, mountains, and back roads which might lead who knows where. She has a weakness for lasagne, garlic bread, tacos, cheese, and chocolate, but not necessarily in that order.
Facebook: GabriellaBalcom.lonestarauthor

The Best Revenge
by Mikko Rauhala

Rob woke up to a splitting headache. As he struggled up, he noticed a tablet screen saying, "Play me", the letters shining bright against the pitch black. He fumbled at the device and was greeted by a contemptuous frown.

"Hi, Rob. Rohypnol's a bitch, right?"

"No, Lisa, you are," Rob snarled. Had his lay gotten him back somehow?

"Should've pleaded guilty," Lisa said. "But now, you know what they say about the best revenge?"

Rob glanced around in the light of the tablet. A circular stone wall surrounded him.

The screen went dark as Lisa's voice uttered: "Live in well."

Mikko Rauhala is a Finnish author of speculative fiction with a national Atorox award nomination under his belt. Informed by his master's degree in intelligent systems, Rauhala is most at home in hard science fiction settings, though he's not exclusive and likes to cross genres. Rauhala has dabbled in editing flash fiction for The Self-Inflicted Relative anthology, and some of his English science fiction can be found in the Infinite Metropolis short story and audio drama collection, co-authored with Edmund Schluessel.
Blog: rauhala.org
Podcast: infinitemetropolis.com

The Illustrated Boy
by Nicola Currie

In Bradbury's stories, the man's tattoos tell the future. Mine tell the past. I'm no artist and they're taking a lot of time, pain, scratched in with a shard of glass, a crafting blade, a razor.

Stroking whatever part of me she's bruised, Mum always slurs that she is proud to have such a beautiful son. So I scar my skin with words like 'beaten,' 'broken,' 'unloved,' drawings of teardrops, stitches, fists.

But 'bitch' was the first word, on the cheek she last stroked, so she'll know it's because of her, when they find my body. I hope it stings.

Nicola Currie is from Cambridge, UK where she works in educational publishing. She has published poetry in literary magazines, including Mslexia and Sarasvati, and short stories in various anthologies. She has also completed her first novel, which was longlisted for the Bath Children's Novel Award. Website: writeitandweep.home.blog

Tea for Two
by Jason Holden

Passed over by the boys' club again! They gave the job to Simon Stone because his father holds some title or some such.

I could have lived with that. Got my head down, worked harder than the boys to earn my place at the top, if I hadn't overheard the C.E.O saying, "She should stick to making tea. It's what women are good at."

I made the tea alright, with a little water hemlock in it to teach those bastards a lesson. I smiled when I gave it to them. Sweet as sugar, while they died on their glass ceiling.

Jason Holden is a human. He lives here and there in the UK, always with his wife, daughter and fur baby. His primary goal is to raise his daughter to adulthood without any major damage. When he can, he writes. He thinks he does it well, but you can be the judge of that. He has been published in a few anthologies here and there, has been praised and put down for his writing. You can find and follow him on Facebook, although he asks you only follow him on Facebook and not through the streets. That's just creepy.
Facebook: Jason Holden-Author

The Press Are Vultures
by Ximena Escobar

Curved like burnt steel on the hot earth, the slight movement of her ribs is the only indication that she's still alive; that and the vulture behind her; still waiting.

Uncaptured are the armed boys behind Kevin; and every other picture he ever took instead of running to aid the dying; tyres burning around their necks, dented bin-lids rattling on the ground.

Sometimes, they wake.

Kevin digs with scavenger talons; he is a vulture too. But there is no salvation, and no grave to rest in. Only the oozing pool that feeds him. Only his repulsive reflection in the blood.

Ximena Escobar is writing stories and poetry. Originally from Chile, she is the author of a translation into Spanish of the Broadway Musical "The Wizard of Oz", and of an original adaptation of the same, "Navidad en Oz", both produced in her home country. Since 2018 she has published several short stories in various anthologies and online platforms, and is now slowly working on her own collection. Ximena has a degree in Arts & Communication Science and lives in Nottingham with her family.
Facebook: Ximenautora
Twitter: @laximenin

Last Laugh
by Shelly Jarvis

You didn't mean to kill them. At least, that's what you keep telling yourself. So why are you smiling?

Was it because the blood seemed to ooze out, gentle and flowing and warm, like lava down the peaks and valleys of her body? Was it the sweet song of your blade as it sang through the air, through his skin? Or was it just the satisfaction of revenge?

For that is what you're happiest about, isn't it? You finally got revenge for the way your heart was crushed beneath their feet.

They laughed at you. But they're not laughing now.

Shelly Jarvis is a speculative fiction author from West Virginia, US. She found a life-long love of sci-fi and fantasy in the 3rd grade when she found Madeleine L'Engle's "A Wrinkle in Time." Shelly is an avid reader, a Whovian, the ideal viewer of dog rescue videos, and undoubtedly Ravenclaw. She currently has three YA sci-fi books available for purchase on Amazon. Website: www.ShellyJarvis.com

Secret Ingredient
by K.B. Elijah

The woman's nostrils flared as she glowered across the table at her greatest enemy, a lump of bitter hatred lodging in her dry throat. Her fingers twitched, uncomfortable with their proximity.

She'd never felt resentment for any person as much as she did for that...loathsome thing, an abomination of the foulest degree. Yet despite its apparent obliviousness to the woman's unceasing contempt, it seemed to haunt her. Barely a day went past without her encountering its putrid presence.

The man seated across from her frowned. "Do you have a problem with my soup?"

"Yes," she snarled. "There's coriander in it!"

K.B. Elijah *is a fantasy author living in Brisbane, Australia with her husband and three cockatiels. A lawyer by day, and a writer by...also day, because she needs her solid nine hours of sleep per night (not that the cockatiels let her sleep past 6am). K.B. writes for various international anthologies, and her work features in dozens of collections about the mysterious, the magical and the macabre. Her own books of short fantasy novellas with twists, The Empty Sky and Out of the Nowhere, are available on paperback and Kindle now.*
Website: www.kbelijah.com
Instagram: k.b.elijah

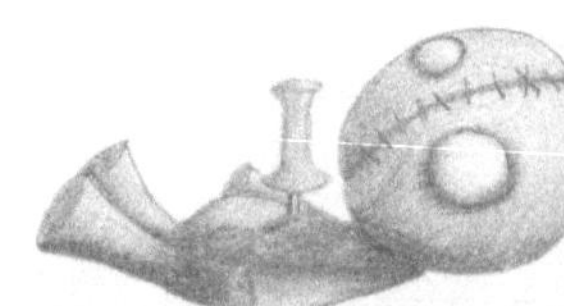

Us and Them
by Dawn Knox

We shuffle towards the entrance; shoulders hunched, eyes avoiding contact with our captors.

Women clutch men.

Children cling to women.

Slowly, we stumble towards the communal showers.

That's what everyone believes.

But I know different. I've studied history and I know the showerheads won't deliver water.

They won't dispense liquid at all.

I make eye contact with the guard. How can another being not be touched by the starved, broken line of humanity it's propelling towards destruction?

Then I know.

Like the men these monsters seek to emulate, they share a hatred of anyone who's not the same as them.

Dawn Knox enjoys writing in different genres and has had romances, speculative fiction, sci-fi, humorous and women's fiction published in magazines, anthologies and books. She's also had two plays about World War One performed internationally. Her current work in progress is a story set in Bletchley Park during World War Two.
Website: dawnknox.com
Twitter: SunriseCalls

Curse
by A.R. Johnston

Was I really going to do this? Was I ready to take the karma, the smut on my soul to do this? Was he really worth it? Tears spilled down her face, staining the wedding photo in her hands. She sniffed, wiped her face with her sleeve, looking up to the person standing in front of her.

"Once you do this, there is no going back. It will stain your soul, but you will have your revenge," the dark voice spoke.

She blinked. "Yes, this is what I want."

"Then place the photo in the fire and let us begin."

A.R. Johnston is a small-town girl from Nova Scotia, Canada. She is known to write mostly urban fantasy, though she goes where the muses lead her and you never know where that may be. She is a lover of coffee, good tv shows, horror flicks, and a reader of good books. She pretends to be a writer when real life doesn't get in the way. Pesky full-time job and adulting!
Facebook: arjohnstonauthor
Website: arjohnstonauthor.wordpress.com

Breathe
by Michele Freeman

Remember what you used to say? *Quit crying, for christsake. Take a breath.*

Not easy to do after you cracked my ribs.

Love? Yeah, right. Your fists created tattoos of your so-called love.

Black eyes.

Bruised skin.

Broken bones.

Your words hurt, too. Shattered my soul with the same force you shattered my body. You hated that I found the courage to walk away.

No, I won't untie you. Stop yelling. We're in the middle of nowhere.

What am I going to do with this hammer? I'm gonna hit you with it. Starting with the ribs. Now…

Take a breath.

Award-winning author **Michele Freeman** *writes horror and dark fiction. She loves crochet, chocolate, and zombies. She lives in Texas with her Viking husband and their adorable fur babies.*
Website: www.authormichelefreeman.com

Home Run
by Dawn DeBraal

The Blue Jays hated the Cardinals. They had a better baseball diamond and sponsors. The Cardinals had official-looking jerseys while the Blue Jays had to hand number their shirts with a sharpie marker.

The Cardinals hated the Blue Jays because they wore crappy shirts, and they never had snacks at their games, and they always won at baseball.

The mothers and fathers of the Blue Jay and Cardinals hated each other. They all showed up at the field one day with bags of baseball bats no one thought to bring a ball. So, they started swinging at one another instead.

Dawn DeBraal lives in rural Wisconsin with her husband Red, two rat terriers, and a cat. She has discovered that her love of telling a good story can be written. Published stories with Palm-sized press, Spillwords, Mercurial Stories, Potato Soup Journal, Edify Fiction, Zimbell House Publishing, Clarendon House Publishing, Blood Song Books, Black Hare Press, Fantasia Divinity, Cafelit, Reanimated Writers, Guilty Pleasures, Unholy Trinity, The World of Myth, Dastaan World, Vamp Cat, Runcible Spoon, Dark Christmas, Siren's Call, Iron Horse Publishing, Falling Star Magazine 2019 Pushcart Nominee.
Amazon: amazon.com/Dawn-DeBraal/e/B07STL8DLX

People Just Gotta Learn the Rules
by Stephen Herczeg

"God damn it," Doug shouted as a car narrowly missed his front fender, "Learn the rules."

He tail-gated it, fuming at the idiotic driver.

It's a simple rule. Give way to any other driver on the roundabout. *Why does everybody think it's give way to the right? Stupid idiots.*

Next day in his new V8 truck, complete with steel bull-bar, Doug entered the empty roundabout. A car accelerated from the right.

Instead of braking, Doug hit the gas. The bull-bar sent the car careering into a wall.

Unrepentant, Doug explained to the dumbfounded police.

"People just gotta learn the rules."

Stephen Herczeg is an IT Geek based in Canberra Australia. He has been writing for over twenty years and has completed a couple of dodgy novels, sixteen feature length screenplays and numerous short stories and scripts. His horror work has featured in Sproutlings, Hells Bells, Below the Stairs, Trickster's Treats #1 and #2, Shades of Santa, Behind the Mask, Beyond the Infinite; The Body Horror Book, Anemone Enemy, Petrified Punks and Beginnings. He has also had numerous Sherlock Holmes stories published through the Belanger Books - Sherlock Holmes anthologies.
Amazon: amazon.com/-/e/B07916SQQS
Facebook: stephenherczegauthor

Target of Hate
by Tracy Davidson

I pick my vantage point, set my sights. No-one notices me. No-one ever notices me.

The object of my hatred comes into view. Betrayal is an ugly thing. It doesn't matter how small or large the betrayal is. Without trust, without honour, what is there?

I don't enjoy my hatred. I never asked for it. Ironically, I hate it.

Hate is invasive. It latches on to your insides. It grows, spreads, festers. Given enough time, it destroys a person's soul. Unless...unless it's allowed out to play.

I let mine out today. On a grassy knoll in Dallas. November, 1963.

Tracy Davidson lives in Warwickshire, England, and writes poetry and flash fiction. Her work has appeared in various publications and anthologies, including: Poet's Market, Mslexia, Atlas Poetica, Writing Magazine, Modern Haiku, The Binnacle, A Hundred Gourds, Shooter, Journey to Crone, The Great Gatsby Anthology, WAR and In Protest: 150 Poems for Human Rights.

Melanie's Choice
by Lynne Phillips

The identical twins had opposite tastes. Melanie loved pretty dresses and dolls. Madeline preferred trousers and toy guns. Melanie would throw a tantrum if she didn't get to choose. When they were young, Madeline resented her sister but complied.

As teenagers, Melanie woke early and played Jazz. Madeline preferred Heavy Metal and sleeping late. Madeline's resentment festered, she vehemently hated her sister and planned to be free of her control forever.

As she plunged a knife into her sleeping sister, the realised as a conjoined twin that was not her best idea and once again Melanie would get to choose.

Lynne Phillips, a retired teacher, lives in the beautiful Northern Rivers Region of New South Wales Australia. Her stories, across all genres, have been published in anthologies and various online magazines. Her priority is spending time with her family. Her passions are reading, writing and keeping fit.

Pincushion
by Brian Rosenberger

He loves me. He loves me not.

A silly game we played as children to determine if our home room crushes cared for us the way we cared for them.

He loves me…

Alex and I loved each other. We told each other daily. A constant reminder. For almost seven years.

Until we didn't. Alex became distant. Alex said he loved another. She was his soulmate.

He told me the same once.

He loves me not…

I stick the needle into the tiny doll till my hand hurts, praying it pains his soul as much as he has pained mine.

***Brian Rosenberger** lives in a cellar in Marietta, GA (USA) and writes by the light of captured fireflies. He is the author of As the Worms Turns and three poetry collections. He is also a featured contributor to the Pro-Wrestling literary collection, Three-Way Dance, available from Gimmick Press.*
Facebook: HeWhoSuffers

Copycat
by V. Mylynne Smith

Nancy, my coworker, was obsessed with me. She permed her hair to look like mine. Her spray tanned skin mirrored my own. The acrylic nails on her fingers were identical to mine. She wanted to take my place. I loathed her for it.

Nancy's house erupted into flames…after I poured gas on it and struck a match. I duct taped Nancy to the front seat of her car while her family burned. I dropped a brick onto the gas pedal and watched her ram into the hydrant nearest her house.

They took me away in cuffs, but I kept laughing.

*V. **Mylynne Smith** primarily writes thrillers, but sometimes dips a toe into horror. Her love of psychology helps her craft malicious characters with the worst intentions. She aims to create twists and turns that keep the reader guessing until the end. Smith is an Oklahoman that moved to Northwest Arkansas after meeting her husband. The pair live together in a cozy house with two pets: a pitbull named Renegade and a feisty cat named Bandit. When Smith isn't stringing words together, you can find her in front of a mirror with make-up in hand or baking something delicious and fattening.*

Revenge is Sweet
by Terri A. Arnold

I would say they're going to live to regret the things they've done to me, but to be honest, none of them are going to survive what I've got planned. They tortured me for years and I will return the favour. I have it all worked out, I will kidnap and torture them one at a time. They'll know I'm coming for them, but they won't know when; they'll spend their days terrified, just as I did. I'll give myself time to enjoy the torture I plan to inflict on them, I vow to be the last person they see.

Terri A. Arnold is an avid reader turned writer from a small town in Nova Scotia, who has spent her life reading and wishing she was writing. Although she has written a lot in those years, she has only recently begun to submit pieces for publication. With ongoing encouragement from family and writing challenges with friends, Arnold felt the urge to try her hand at publishing.

The Porcupine Man
by Terry Miller

Roses are red, blood's the same hue. Thorns are prickly, now he is too.

Gail watched Vince's terrified eyes, tears tracing his flushed cheeks. How many pores are there in the human body? Perhaps she could fill each one; pores that oozed sweat as he slept with her sister, Tammy. *Sewing needles weren't just for sewing anymore,* she entertained.

The trickling crimson streams dripped to the bedsheets; perhaps she'd created a new artform. Vince drifted between awake and asleep, his autonomic nervous system in a frantic fit. Gail smiled as the colour slowly faded from his cheeks. *Suffering is life.*

Terry Miller *lives in Portsmouth, Ohio. His work has been featured in Sanitarium Magazine, Devolution Z, Jitter, Rhysling Anthology 2017, Poetry Quarterly, Sirens Call Ezine, The Horror Tree's Trembling With Fear, SpillWords, Organic Ink Vol. I, Curses & Cauldrons Anthology from Blood Song Books, Forest of Fear from Blood Song Books, the Dark Drabble Anthology Series from Black Hare Press, 100 Word Zombie Bites from Reanimated Writers Press, Scary Snippets, Guilty Pleasures & Other Dark Delights, 100 Word Horrors 3, and O Unholy Night In Deathlehem from Grinning Skull Press.*
Facebook: tmiller2015
Amazon: amazon.com/author/millerterryl

Ashes in the Water
by G. Allen Wilbanks

Donald stood as close to the cliffside as he dared, staring out over the waves crashing against the rocks below. He held out the metal urn containing his wife's ashes and unfastened the lid.

When the sun touched the water at the horizon and the wind was blowing just right, he upended the urn, casting his wife's mortal remains to their final resting place. As he watched the ashes scatter and dance on the eddies of wind on their way into the vast ocean before him, Donald smiled.

He thought to himself, *that bitch was always terrified of the water.*

G. Allen Wilbanks *is a member of the Horror Writers Association (HWA) and has published over 100 short stories in various magazines and on-line venues. He is the author of two short story collections, and the novel, When Darkness Comes. Website: www.gallenwilbanks.com Blog: DeepDarkThoughts.com*

Hate Versus Love
by Olivia Arieti

Kelly had to decide whether she loved Ross more than she hated him. It wasn't easy; if hate prevailed, she was determined to kill him. His absence was devastating, but his affair with her best friend unforgivable. She even considered eliminating the rival, but it wouldn't be as gratifying as seeing her husband agonising at her feet.

It didn't matter if the bastard repented and cried, "Better dead than without you."

Ironically, his words had triggered the murderous thought.

While one emotion was finally choking the other, she put the revolver in her bag and headed towards their final rendezvous.

Olivia Arieti has a degree from the University of Pisa and lives in Torre del Lago Puccini, Italy, with her family. Besides being a published playwright, she loves writing retellings of fairy tales, and at the same time is intrigued by supernatural and horror themes. Her stories appeared in several magazines and anthologies like Enchanted Conversations, Enchanted Tales Literary Magazine, Fantasia Divinity Magazine, Cliterature, Medieval Nightmares, Static Movement, 100 Doors To Madness Forgotten Tomb Press, Black Cats Horrified Press, Bloody Ghost Stories Full Moon Books, Death And Decorations Thirteen O'Clock Press, Infective Ink, Pandemonium Press, Pussy Magic Magazine.

Have a Nice Fall
by Clint Foster

His face is practically purple as he screams at me, veins throbbing in his temples and neck. Today is the day. I had decided. No more working for a man who degrades me, who tears me down, who sees all the bad in me and never even a sliver of the good. Today is the day he learns just how bad I can be.

He finishes and I smile, devoid of my last grain of patience.

"What're you grinning at, you—"

I can imagine what he would've called me, but the fall from his fiftieth floor window shuts him up.

Clint Foster lives with his herd of four cats, beloved Basset, Zero, and wonderful wife, Nik. He loves to tell stories just as much as he loves to read them, and is excited to share his work. A longtime consumer of media of all kinds, he enjoys giving back what he hopes everyone else thinks are good stories. Facebook: *ClintFosterAuthor*

Love Me Once
by Umair Mirxa

Lucien pushed Katelyn up against the wall and placed a palm across her mouth to keep her quiet.

"Why couldn't you choose me?" he snarled in her ear, resting his forehead against a tear-stained cheek. "All you had to do was love me once. Instead, you've turned *my* feelings for you into this…this ugly hatred I cannot control."

He ignored her muted pleas and desperate whimpers as he fiddled with his belt and drew, with difficulty, the dagger there.

"I would have kept you happy, you know?" he said, now abruptly calm even as he slit her throat open.

Umair Mirxa lives and writes in Karachi, Pakistan. His first published story, 'Awareness', appeared on Spillwords Press. He has since had stories accepted for publication in anthologies from Zombie Pirate Publishing, Blood Song Books, Black Hare Press, Iron Faerie Publishing, Clarendon House Publications, Fantasia Divinity Magazine & Publishing, and The ReAnimated Writers Press. He is a massive J.R.R. Tolkien fan, loves everything to do with mythology, fantasy, and history, and wishes with all his heart that dragons were real. When he's not writing, he enjoys reading novels and comic books, playing video games, listening to music, and watching movies, TV shows, and football as an Arsenal FC fan.
Website: umairmirxa.com

She Even Took My Hand Cream
by Stephen Herczeg

I can't believe it, my seat's not even cold.

That loud, horrible woman took my seat, my desk, my cupboard. That screeching voice, it never stopped. Every day, from clock on till home time. Never ending. Grating on my mind. There were days I just wanted to stick knives in my ears.

I always knew she wanted my window desk. The view was to die for, but I never meant it literally.

Now I'm stuck. I can still hear her. I will make her pay. I'll haunt her dreams or something.

Oh, come on, she even took my hand cream.

Stephen Herczeg is an IT Geek based in Canberra Australia. He has been writing for over twenty years and has completed a couple of dodgy novels, sixteen feature length screenplays and numerous short stories and scripts. His horror work has featured in Sproutlings, Hells Bells, Below the Stairs, Trickster's Treats #1 and #2, Shades of Santa, Behind the Mask, Beyond the Infinite; The Body Horror Book, Anemone Enemy, Petrified Punks and Beginnings. He has also had numerous Sherlock Holmes stories published through the Belanger Books - Sherlock Holmes anthologies.
Amazon: amazon.com/-/e/B07916SQQS
Facebook: stephenherczegauthor

Janus Lot's Wife
by Paula R.C. Readman

"What's the answer to the riddle of the sentinels?" my wife snarled, while staring at the stone circle.

I shrugged, knowing once she became wolfish with a bone between her teeth, silence was best.

"You've no balls!" she barked.

I realised her conversation wasn't about the stones.

"Too busy looking backwards, aren't you?"

She's right. I began to walk away, a peaceful life awaited me.

"Hey, come back here, Janus Lot?"

As I drove away, she became rigid with anger that I'd left. Not quite a pillar of salt, but enough to leave a nasty taste in her nagging mouth.

Paula R.C. Readman learnt 'How to Write' from books which her husband purchased from eBay. After 250 purchases, he finally told her 'just to get on with the writing'. Since 2010, she's had 34 stories published.
Blog: *paulareadman1.wordpress.com*

The Plunge
by J.M. Ames

You won't know what happened. The air will be crisp with autumn and salted by the Pacific. Spray from the waves that will batter the pylons will dance and swirl about your feet as you meander to the fate that will await you. Perhaps you will hear the footsteps behind you at the last second, perhaps not. Either way, you will realise what is happening when her gloved hands plunge the knife into your spine and shove you over the railing. Her cries of your eternal damnation will fill your ears, and then the seawater will as well. Then darkness.

J.M. Ames is an award-winning multi-genre speculative fiction author native to Southern California. He has multiple short story publications dating back to 2016. One thing holds true throughout all of his stories - you can Expect the Unexpected. When not working his day job or enjoying his fatherly adventures, he writes short stories and novels, including an upcoming series. You can follow him on a variety of platforms, details on his website.
Website: jm-ames.com/contact-jm/

Hell Hath No Fury Like a Psychopath Scorned
by Frances Tate

Your mouth crinkles into that devastating smile. Origami in petals. Lips blossom like a rose. The sight steals moisture from my mouth to sustain it. Raises heartbeat, temperature and the need to take you in this crowded bar.

Don't think your date would approve. Prim prude. She hasn't responded to music or the effect of your oh-so-talented mouth. I looked her up. She's minted, Daddy's sole heir. Has a decade and a dowry over me.

Let's see if she can outdo me in life lessons.

You see me, eyes open wide. Face pales. Panics.

I watch fear devastate your smile.

Frances Tate is a British self-published writer of vampires and drabbles who lives in the north west of England. She enjoys gardening, exploring historical sites, cinema, reading and travelling. She's taken pleasure in flight-planning a cabbage white butterfly approach to careers, preferring to generalise rather than specialise. She trained as an Economics high school teacher and has a private pilot's licence amongst other things. Currently she writes (very restrained) overhaul instructions for an engineering company.

Liar
by Catherine Kenwell

"You told me you could never sleep with anyone you didn't love."

"Well, yeah, but…"

"So you slept with me. In my bed. Imagine me, thinking you loved me. What a fool!"

"That was different—"

"And now you say, 'you never loved me like I thought you did'. Go figure."

"Well, no, that's—"

"That's what you SAID!"

"I'm sorry."

"You're not sorry."

"Listen, I *like* you…"

"Tell me. Say it: I. LOVE. YOU."

"OK, I *love* you."

"Liar."

I reach into my purse. Pull out a Smith & Wesson.

"If there's one thing I hate, it's a liar."

Catherine Kenwell is a Barrie, Ontario, mediator and author. After 30 successful years in corporate communications, she sustained a brain injury, lost her job, and joined the circus. She writes both horror/dark fiction and inspirational non-fiction. Her works have been published in Chicken Soup for the Soul, Trembling with Fear, Siren's Call, and HellBound Books. Website: www.catherinekenwell.com

A Growing Alarm
by Maxine Churchman

I didn't hate him at first. He was pathetic; strutting in front of the class, exalting in the power he held over us. Then he became annoying; using the most tenuous of reasons to detain me.

I ignored him when he hailed me in the High Street; that was just creepy.

His habit of rubbing his thighs when he talked to me was repellent, but I only began to dislike him after realising his eyes followed me everywhere.

Then he trapped me; pressed himself against me. I did hate him then; why else would I have stabbed him—twenty times?

Maxine Churchman lives in Essex UK and has recently started writing poetry and short stories to share. Her interests include learning to improve her writing, reading, knitting, walking and teaching yoga. She is also planning a novel.

In Time
by Brianna Witte

Thief. Liar. Traitor.

The words clung to the tip of my tongue ready to explode out of my mouth. She spoke, giving me that fake, sarcastic smile that she always did. Her words were inaudible against my fierce heartbeat.

Hatred oozed out of my pores. Hatred for what she had done; hatred for the arrogance and ruthless isolation she had given me over the past few months.

I bit my lip, stopping myself from blurting out my true feelings towards her. The time would come when I would finally be free of her. Revenge was waiting just around the corner.

*As an up and coming writer from Ontario, Canada, **Brianna Witte** has a passion for spinning tales of adventure and fantasy. She enjoys taking readers on a ride through the realm of fiction by weaving magical and mystical stories that materialise from her wildly creative dreams and vivid imagination. To date she has had a number of short stories and drabbles published, as well as her short story, 'The Hunt' commended for the 2019 Author of Tomorrow award. She also had a novel, Witches and Vampires, published in December 2019.*
Facebook: BriannaWitteAuthor
Instagram: briannawitteauthor

A Lesson in Trust
by Paula R.C. Readman

The light shone bright in her eyes as she laid them on the table.

The count wasn't sure he could compete with her, but love drives you to do many crazy things. He removed his teeth—a sign of trust—and gave a gummy smile.

She brushed her cold lips against his, and with a sigh, she whispered, "What the eyes don't see, the heart doesn't grieve."

"But my dear…" he said, puzzled until the stake entered his heart.

As the dust swirled around her, she popped her eyes back saying, "I hope that teaches you, never trust a scorned woman."

***Paula R.C. Readman** learnt 'How to Write' from books which her husband purchased from eBay. After 250 purchases, he finally told her 'just to get on with the writing'. Since 2010, she's had 34 stories published.*
Blog: paulareadman1.wordpress.com

Smile For Me
by J.W. Garrett

The shiny instruments lay on the table, the chair reclined. A drowsy man waited, uncertain of his fate. While I wasn't exactly sure how to proceed, years of experience at this man's hand with hideous results gave me insight to the painful first steps.

Patience was my friend.

I flashed the long needle before him, pressed down slightly on the plunger, before slowly injecting the placebo medication into the roof of his mouth. Writhing in his seat, he was unable to scream.

"Four more of those, then I'll *attempt* to extract your gum tissue and see which teeth remain. *Smile.*"

J.W. Garrett has been writing in one form or another since she was a teenager. She currently lives in Florida with her family but loves the mountains of Virginia where she was born. Her writings include YA fantasy as well as short stories. Since completing Remeon's Quest-Earth Year 1930, the prequel in her YA fantasy series, Realms of Chaos, she has been hard at work on the next in the series, scheduled to release August 2020. When she's not hanging out with her characters, her favourite activities are reading, running and spending time with family.
Website: www.jwgarrett.com
BHC Press: www.bhcpress.com/Author_JW_Garrett.html

Murder She Wrote
by Umair Mirxa

Mahesh screamed and shed tears of blood, writhing in agony as Claire pulled the blunt, rusted knife out. Both his eyeballs had been punctured.

"There," she said with grim satisfaction, kneeling to better inspect her handiwork. "You can't steal what you cannot see. I trusted you bastards, you know!"

She stood and kicked him in the groin before taking a seat on the sofa. The beta-reading, good-for-nothing scumbags had plagiarised her entire novel, down to the last word.

"I will kill your wife when she returns, and write a brand new novel based upon your murders here tonight," said Claire.

Umair Mirxa lives and writes in Karachi, Pakistan. His first published story, 'Awareness', appeared on Spillwords Press. He has since had stories accepted for publication in anthologies from Zombie Pirate Publishing, Blood Song Books, Black Hare Press, Iron Faerie Publishing, Clarendon House Publications, Fantasia Divinity Magazine & Publishing, and The ReAnimated Writers Press. He is a massive J.R.R. Tolkien fan, loves everything to do with mythology, fantasy, and history, and wishes with all his heart that dragons were real. When he's not writing, he enjoys reading novels and comic books, playing video games, listening to music, and watching movies, TV shows, and football as an Arsenal FC fan.
Website: umairmirxa.com

Turned Up to Eleven
by Clint Foster

"Don't turn it up past eight, you know the speakers are sensitive."

As if I haven't heard him say it a thousand times. Except this time, I won't stop at eight. Nine, ten, eleven, twelve. The dial goes up to twenty-five, and I crank it higher and higher while he protests, lunging across the living room with a raised hand aimed not for the dial, but my cheek. It isn't the first time, but it will be the last. He couldn't have seen the knife in my hand. The speakers blow out just in time for his screaming to start.

Clint Foster lives with his herd of four cats, beloved Basset, Zero, and wonderful wife, Nik. He loves to tell stories just as much as he loves to read them, and is excited to share his work. A longtime consumer of media of all kinds, he enjoys giving back what he hopes everyone else thinks are good stories.
Facebook: ClintFosterAuthor

Burning in the Night
by Destiny Eve Pifer

In the darkness, she flicks the lighter and watches the flame dance against the cool night air. Beside her, a muffled cry can be heard, but she knows it is a pain they must endure.

She glares to her side, at the man fighting against the masking tape, but it's too late to turn back time. Too late to erase the pain he has caused her.

The smell of lighter fluid fills her nostrils, and she closes her eyes and sighs. She reaches over and gently runs the flame across his arm until his whole body erupts into a blaze.

Destiny Eve Pifer *is a published author whose work has appeared in numerous anthologies and magazines. Her stories have been featured in FATE Magazine, True Confessions, Spotlight on Recovery and Country Magazine. A lover of all things supernatural and spooky she resides in Punxsutawney, Pennsylvania with her son Dartanyan.*

Infamous Last Words
by John H. Dromey

"Sylvia was the victim of a vicious hate crime," the lead detective announced. "Jealousy was the motive."

"Based on what?" someone asked.

"This bloodstained printout pinned to her breast with a stiletto. The e-mail she sent in reply to a mushy message from a new lover. It says, 'I love you, two.' Spelled *t-w-o*. The obvious conclusion is Sylvia wanted a *ménage à trois* and the new man was unhappy with the arrangement. He wanted exclusivity."

"Sylvia wasn't cheating. No *Cc* was sent, and her other e-mails are all filled with typos."

"The killer didn't know that…misprints are murder."

John H. Dromey was born in northeast Missouri, USA. He enjoys reading—mysteries in particular—and writing in a variety of genres. In addition to contributing to the Black Hare Press series of Dark Drabbles anthologies, he's had short fiction published in Alfred Hitchcock's Mystery Magazine, Martian Magazine, Mystery Weekly, Stupefying Stories Showcase, Thriller Magazine, Unfit Magazine, and elsewhere, as well as in numerous anthologies, including Chilling Horror Short Stories (Flame Tree Publishing, 2015).

Left at the Altar
by Evelyn Benvie

Shendae lay her infant daughter on the slab. The child went quietly. She was such a good girl.

Nothing like her father.

No, nothing like him. He was all fuss and noise, angry words and broken promises. But he would learn; how to be silent, how to be still.

A slip of jezebel root tucked in the swaddle. A boneset candle, already lit. A black iron dagger forged only in moonlight.

Everything Shendae needed to curse that good-for-nothing ex of hers.

Almost everything.

The only thing she was missing was something of his.

The blood of his child would do.

Evelyn Benvie is the wooly jumper in a family of black sheep. Both a cynic and a romantic at heart, she writes diverse, queer-positive fiction and poetry that have been published online and in print. Her first novella, Something to Celebrate, was recently published by Mischief Corner Books and is available on Amazon.
Website: evelynbenvie.com
Twitter: EvelynBenvie

The Last Straw
by Jodi Jensen

Helen followed her husband's mistress all day as the woman picked up his prescriptions, mailed his packages, and stopped at the store for his favourite bottle of wine.

All things Helen used to do for him.

The last straw was when the woman pulled up in front of the laundromat.

Through the window, Helen saw her husband inside, folding his lover's panties.

In thirty-nine years of marriage, he'd never once done that for her.

She slammed the pedal to the floor, ramming into the other car and sending his mistress through the windshield.

First time Helen had smiled in years.

Jodi Jensen, author of time travel romances and speculative fiction short stories, grew up moving from California, to Massachusetts, and a few other places in between, before finally settling in Utah at the ripe old age of nine. The nomadic life fed her sense of adventure as a child and the wanderlust continues to this day. With a passion for old cemeteries, historical buildings and sweeping sagas of days gone by, it was only natural she'd dream of time traveling to all the places that sparked her imagination.
Twitter: @WritesJodi
Facebook: jodijensenwrites

The Weave
by Maura Yzmore

At first, we rejoiced at the newcomers' arrival.

We had always been alone, interwoven, a gentle silent web within the sea. Beneath us, the laminae of our ancestors, never truly gone or forgotten. The sea, pulsating with our thoughts, past and present as one.

But the newcomers sought something; what, we did not know. Their machines, hard and loud, drilling, piercing our weave, disrespectful.

Our ancestors yielded, just enough.

Enough to trap.

Enough to let the sea make all hard things soft and all loud things quiet.

We are alone once again, interwoven, a gentle silent web within the sea.

Maura Yzmore is a writer and science professor based in the American Midwest. Some of her darker fare can be found in The Molotov Cocktail, Aphotic Realm, Coffin Bell, and elsewhere. Website: maurayzmore.com
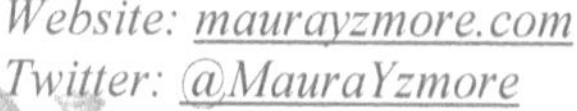
Twitter: @MauraYzmore

Trapped
by Annie Percik

He left me. He left me here to take the blame. He left me here to take the blame for his crime. But I'll get out. One day, I'll get out of here. One day, I'll get out of here and I'll track him down. Then he'll be sorry. He'll be sorry he ever laid eyes on me. He'll be sorry he ever laid eyes on me, and he'll learn that he underestimated me. Everything he has ever loved will be destroyed. He'll be left to suffer his losses. Just like he left me to suffer here in his place.

Annie Percik lives in London with her husband, Dave, where she is revising her first novel whilst working as a University Complaints Officer. She writes a blog about writing and posts short fiction on her website, which is also where all her current publications are listed. She also publishes a photo-story blog, recording the adventures of her teddy—he is much more popular online than she is. She likes to run away from zombies in her spare time.
Website: www.alobear.co.uk
Blog: aloysius-bear.dreamwidth.org/

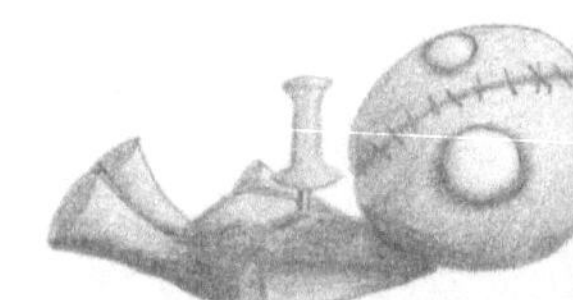

Calista
by Vonnie Winslow Crist

When Calista needed a chihuahua for a costume party, she bought one. Then, she sashayed in her pink ensemble to the event carrying the pup in her purse. Next day, she dropped the dog off at the animal shelter.

"Does she have her shots?" asked Jess when Calista handed her the chihuahua.

"Don't know. Don't care."

Jess comforted the shivering dog and watched Calista depart.

That night, Jess dumped some fleas she'd gathered from shelter strays through an open window into Calista's house.

Revenge is easier when you live nearby, Jess mused as she thought of a flea-bitten Calista.

Vonnie Winslow Crist is author of The Enchanted Dagger, Owl Light, The Greener Forest, Murder on Marawa Prime, and other award-winning books. Her fiction is included in "Amazing Stories," "Cast of Wonders," "Outposts of Beyond," Killing It Softly 2, Defending the Future - Dogs of War, Midnight Masquerade, Chaos of Hard Clay, and elsewhere. A cloverhand who has found so many four-leafed clovers she keeps them in jars, Vonnie strives to celebrate the power of myth in her writing.
Website: www.vonniewinslowcrist.com

The Apartment
by Trisha Ridinger McKee

Sam packed the last of the boxes into his car and set out toward the new place, relieved he had gotten out of his lease so easily.

He had not seen the new place, but his friends boasted about the spacious rooms, large bay windows, and a spa-like bathroom.

He was ecstatic his friends asked him to move in with them. He had never felt fully part of their group. But now they were going to be roommates.

After thirty minutes, he arrived at the address given…and stared at the abandoned building with broken windows and no trespassing signs.

***Trisha Ridinger McKee** resides in a small town in Pennsylvania where love has proven to be a problem. Her work has appeared or is forthcoming in publications such as Tablet Magazine, The Oddville Press, Crab Fat Literary Magazine, Night to Dawn Magazine, Deep Fried Horror, 4 Star Stories, and more.*

Sweetheart
by Nicola Currie

If he calls me sweetheart one more time…

My boss likes to touch my leg. It's usually a brief squeeze, accompanied by some form of patronising faux reassurance. Today, throughout the corporate lunch, his hand lingers beneath the table.

We are the last two seated as the others return to the boardroom. He moves his hand higher. My steak knife glints.

I don't even mind the blade passing through his hand, nicking my thigh. All I see is his wide-eyed shock, hear his high-pitched scream. I remove the knife and plunge it into his leg.

"There, there, sweetheart. Don't fret."

Nicola Currie is from Cambridge, UK where she works in educational publishing. She has published poetry in literary magazines, including Mslexia and Sarasvati, and short stories in various anthologies. She has also completed her first novel, which was longlisted for the Bath Children's Novel Award. Website: writeitandweep.home.blog

On Reflection
by Maxine Churchman

I see her looking at me. Always staring, mocking my every word and the way I look. She's no great shakes; fat and spotty with lank listless hair. I hate her so much. Not just because of the way she looks but also because of how she makes me feel, because of what I see behind her eyes; the loathing, the vindictiveness, and above all, the pity. I can't stand her pity.

I punch her as hard as I can; right on her big spotty nose. The mirror shatters and my knuckles bleed. I should feel better, but I don't.

Maxine Churchman lives in Essex UK and has recently started writing poetry and short stories to share. Her interests include learning to improve her writing, reading, knitting, walking and teaching yoga. She is also planning a novel.

Monsters
by Chris Bannor

He thought he could stop the hate and show her the truth. Love saw no boundaries, knew no race, colour, or creed. It was all. She had grown up with a legacy of hate though, and he believed he could end her barbaric ways.

He showed patience at her ignorance, understanding at her doubts. He loved and tried to fill the hollows of her heart that had only believed the worst.

When she showed up with an Oak spike and tried to drive it through his heart, he knew better. Hate ended her life as surely as the wooden stake.

Chris Bannor is a science fiction and fantasy writer who lives in Southern California. Chris learned her love of genre stories from her mother at an early age and has never veered far from that path. She also enjoys musical theater and road trips with her family but is a general homebody otherwise.
Facebook: chrisbannorauthor
Website: ChrisBannor.com

Bowline Vengeance
by Michael Carter

"Rabbit pops out of the hole, goes around a tree, under a root blocking the hole, around another tree, back down the hole." Neil muttered the mnemonic while cinching the last bowline knot. The scaly appendages of the hostile intruder were now tied to the ticking bomb.

He stepped back. The creature repeated in fragmented speech: "Rabbit…out hole, around…tree, under…root…down hole."

Neil attempted to move to safety, but something restrained him. He saw tentacles retract to the creature. His face turned pale when he noticed rope tied around his leg, as the final seconds ticked away.

Michael Carter is a short fiction and creative nonfiction writer who grew up reading an odd combination of sci-fi and Louis L'Amour westerns. He's also a lawyer, fly fisherman, and Space Camp alum.

Website; www.michaelcarter.ink
Twitter: mcmichaelcarter

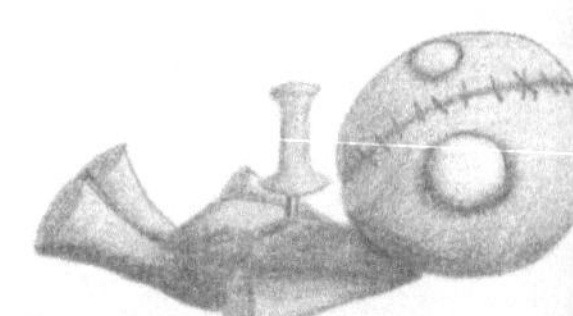

Unconditional
by A.L. King

I never understood that whole *"You love your children unconditionally"* crap. I loathed them as soon as they were born, when they ceased to be one with Eva. The crying, snotting, puking, pissing, and shitting! Only reason we had three was because she wanted them.

They were vampires, except they didn't drink blood. They sucked up our resources and stole our happiness. So when Eva left us, I had to slay them. Only, I used bullets instead of stakes.

Eva doesn't visit, but *they* do. Reborn as ghostly energy vampires, they come from the shadows of my cell to feast.

A.L. King is an author of horror, fantasy, science fiction, and poetry. As an avid fan of dark subjects from an early age, his first influences included R.L. Stine, Edgar Allan Poe, and Stephen King. Later stylistic inspirations came from foreign horror films and media, particularly Japanese. He is a graduate of West Liberty University, has dabbled in journalism, and is actively involved in his community. Although his creativity leans toward darker genres, he has even written a children's book titled "Leif's First Fall." He was raised in the town of Sistersville, West Virginia, which he still proudly calls home.

Helping Hand
by G. Allen Wilbanks

"I think I'm going to die," said Paula. She turned toward the toilet again. Her back arched and her stomach clenched as she wretched and ejected a thin stream of yellow-green bile into the bowl. She spat the bitter fluid from her mouth.

Archie did not comment, he merely held her long, auburn hair away from her face and gently rubbed her back. Paula smiled weakly at him.

"You're being really nice to me right now. Thank you."

"Not a problem," said Archie. "I figured it's the least I could do, especially since I'm the one who poisoned your food."

G. Allen Wilbanks is a member of the Horror Writers Association (HWA) and has published over 100 short stories in various magazines and on-line venues. He is the author of two short story collections, and the novel, When Darkness Comes.
Website: www.gallenwilbanks.com
Blog: DeepDarkThoughts.com

A Victim of Love
by Ann Christine Tabaka

Ever since Janet first met James, she felt like a victim. James came out of nowhere, like a speeding car. His love was like a blinding light; it froze Janet in her tracks. She stood her ground, doe-eyed and afraid to believe that James was real. He came at her full speed ahead and ran her over with his adoring ways. His sugary words and dazzling gifts disguised his true intentions.

Janet wasn't prepared, she didn't stand a chance. She was willing victim, an accident of James's deceiving charm. Now she limps away, trying to find her true self again.

Ann Christine Tabaka was nominated for the 2017 Pushcart Prize in Poetry, has been internationally published, and won poetry awards from numerous publications. She is the author of 9 poetry books. Christine lives in Delaware, USA. She loves gardening and cooking. Chris lives with her husband and two cats. Her most recent credits are: Burningword Literary Journal; Ethos Literary Journal, North of Oxford, Pomona Valley Review, Page & Spine, West Texas Literary Review, The Hungry Chimera, Sheila-Na-Gig, Pangolin Review, Foliate Oak Review, Better Than Starbucks!, The Write Launch, The Stray Branch, The McKinley Review, Fourth & Sycamore.

The Mummy of the Marsh
by Matthew M. Montelione

The mummy stood knee-deep in the marsh. Muddy water dripped from his decaying flesh. He had been jolted from his long watery sleep by the fateful shriek of one of his children. He felt pure hatred.

With all of his power, the mummy summoned his nearby babies. They came in droves, slithering across the wet ground and into the reed-covered waters, oscillating around their master's bandaged legs.

They whispered to him the name of the man who killed their sister.

The mummy let out an agonised groan and left the brackish marshland. He made his way towards the doomed murderer.

Matthew M. Montelione is a horror writer and American Revolution historian born and raised on Long Island in New York. His work has been published in many titles, including MONSTERS: A Horror Microfiction Anthology, Quoth the Raven: A Contemporary Reimagining of the Works of Edgar Allan Poe, Thuggish Itch: Devilish, WHAT IF?: History Rewritten, Long Island History Journal, and Journal of the American Revolution. Matthew lives with his wife in New York.
Website: maybeevils.com
Facebook: maybeevils

Merciless
by Zoey Xolton

The Serpent King held the kidnapped princess in a vice-like grip, a gleaming dagger at her throat.

"Release Elariel, and I will end your life with mercy," promised Vorthax, the princess' First Knight, and protector.

The Serpent King laughed, his body quaking. His hand slipped, nicking the princess' pale flesh, and she whimpered.

Vorthax saw red. Faster than the eye could follow, he threw a small, perfectly weighted knife. It sliced through the air, embedding itself hilt-deep in the Serpent King's eye socket. He fell.

Elariel turned to find her sworn enemy dead.

"That was more mercy than he deserved."

Zoey Xolton is an Australian Speculative Fiction writer, primarily of Dark Fantasy, Paranormal Romance and Horror. She is also a proud mother of two and is married to her soul mate. Outside of her family, writing is her greatest passion. She is especially fond of short fiction and is working on releasing her own themed collections in future.
Website: www.zoeyxolton.com

Laying the Blame
by Annie Percik

She took my teddy. And all she does is lie there and cry. Why should she get to have a teddy? She's drooled all over his fur, too. Now he'll never be the same. She doesn't deserve a teddy of her own. I was here first and she's already taken all of Mummy's attention. It's not fair that she should get my teddy too. That's why I'm going to shut her up once and for all. If she stops crying, maybe Mummy will stop giving her things. All I need is a few minutes alone with her, and a pillow.

Annie Percik lives in London with her husband, Dave, where she is revising her first novel whilst working as a University Complaints Officer. She writes a blog about writing and posts short fiction on her website, which is also where all her current publications are listed. She also publishes a photo-story blog, recording the adventures of her teddy—he is much more popular online than she is. She likes to run away from zombies in her spare time.
Website: www.alobear.co.uk
Blog: aloysius-bear.dreamwidth.org/

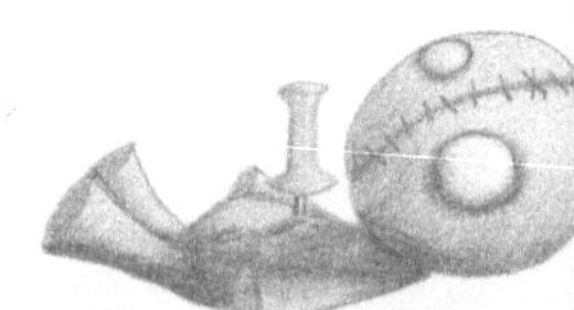

A Life of Hate
by Nerisha Kemraj

When you find yourself backed into a corner,

and all the angry tears have crusted,

blinding you,

when the embers of the burning fire fuelling

your contempt

has died down,

when the ink that writes your turmoil,

drips bloody tears from your sword of fury,

when your thirst for vengeance

has been quenched...

Then,

you realise

that all that's left is hate.

Pure hate,

abandoned by the emotions that drove you

to your downfall,

the hate

that eventually consumes you

into nothingness.

And then you find

there's no one left

to witness your demise,

because

you pushed them all away.

Nerisha Kemraj resides in Durban, South Africa with her husband and two mischievous daughters. Writing since 2017, she has had over 100 short stories and poems published in various publications, both print and online. She has also received an Honourable Mention Award for her tanka in the Fujisan Taisho 2019 Tanka Contest. She holds a Bachelor's degree in Communication Science, and a Post Graduate Certificate in Education from University of South Africa.
Amazon: amazon.com/author/nerisha_kemraj
Facebook: Nerishakemrajwriter

Her Face
by Dermott O'Malley

Every man, woman and child wears her face like a mask. Clouds in the sky and coffee stains on my clothes take her shape. I go to work, building stairs and cutting in doors, and every unfinished piece of pine or cedar where knots in the wood come close to a line, I see her there, too. I stare into the eyes of the wood as I saw it in half; they are as lifeless as her eyes were that day. Hark! Louder! The saw deafens me, but nothing stops the swirls behind my eyelids from showing her to me.

Dermott O'Malley is fascinated by the darker side of life, and his writing often follows suite. He is the author of Thread Count, originally published in Halloween Horror: Volume 1, and reprinted in the anthology, On Time. His second story, a novelette titled Memoirs of a Mute, was published in the anthology Lost Love. He has had other flash pieces and drabbles published in various forms and places.
Twitter: @DermottOMalley

Sweets for My Sweetheart
by Raven Corinn Carluk

Jason counted the orders while the chocolate melted. Three times as many as last Valentine's, almost all requesting some sappy declaration of love.

Including one to his beloved Samantha.

This was finally the year to go full-bore. No playing around with mild irritants and tiny doses of salmonella. Jason would pull out all the best toxins for these shallow fools that thought one day of candy was enough to make up for the rest of the year.

And for sweet Sammie? Arsenic in every bite. She had scorned him for another; Jason would save her from breaking any more hearts.

Raven Corinn Carluk *writes dark fantasy, paranormal romance, and anything else that catches her interest. She's authored five novels, where she explores themes of love and acceptance. Her shorter pieces, usually from her darker side, can be found in Black Hare Press anthologies, at Detritus Online, and through Alban Lake Publishers.*
Twitter: @ravencorinn
Website: www.ravencorinncarluk.com

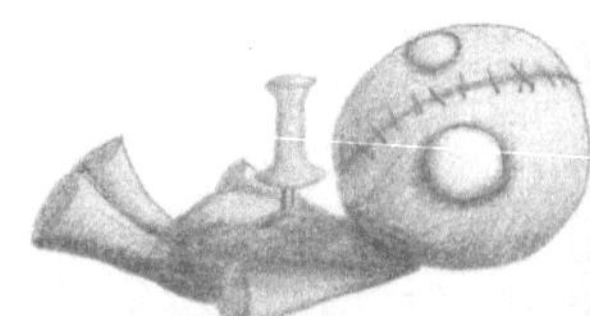

Home Warfare
by D.J. Elton

Three girls were waiting for Andy as he turned the corner, whistling a tune.

"Stop, Boy." Cold words.

A girl with long blonde hair stood in his path, holding a stick.

Become a ninja.

Andy dropped his schoolbag.

"Leave it there," one ordered. He felt nails dig into his clammy skin. *Who are they? They look Angie's age.* Andy was seven.

"You're Angie Bate's brother."

Freeze like a ninja.

"We don't like your sister." Blondie's face looks ugly, jealous.

Thwack. A slap across his head.

And another.

Not fair. Andy passed out and they left him.

Sometimes even ninjas lose.

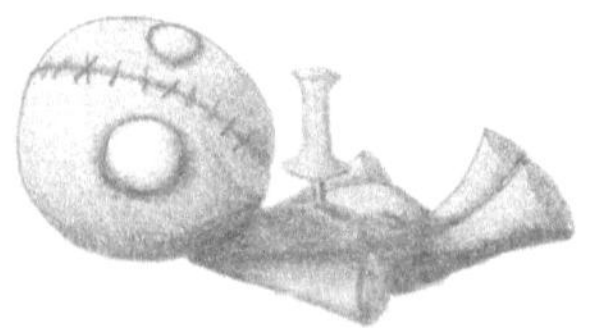

***D.J. Elton** is a writer living in Melbourne's west. As a child she came from England to Australia, on the last boat down the Suez Canal, where she underwent a sacrificial dunking ritual in the court of King Neptune, and has never looked back. She likes creating speculative micro fiction and short stories, as well as random essays. Her work has been published in several anthologies, and she has written a historical fantasy novella, 'The Merlin Girl.' When not playing with a pen, she likes most of all to go to the green country.*

Til Death Do Us Part
by Nerisha Kemraj

Erica jabbed the voodoo doll, savouring Mike's pain.

"Thought you could leave me just like that, did you?" She glared as he fell to the ground, grunting.

"You must hate me now. But that's ok." She twisted the doll's arm, causing Mike to writhe on the floor.

Her laughter accompanied his screams as it rang through the house.

"Sorry, I forgot to mention I was a darkling," she said, stabbing the doll's abdomen as red patterns stained the front of Mike's shirt.

"You're sick," he said through gritted teeth.

"That's better than being dead," she said, lacerating the doll's neck.

Nerisha Kemraj resides in Durban, South Africa with her husband and two mischievous daughters. Writing since 2017, she has had over 100 short stories and poems published in various publications, both print and online. She has also received an Honourable Mention Award for her tanka in the Fujisan Taisho 2019 Tanka Contest. She holds a Bachelor's degree in Communication Science, and a Post Graduate Certificate in Education from University of South Africa.
Amazon: *amazon.com/author/nerisha_kemraj*
Facebook: *Nerishakemrajwriter*

Hate in Half the Time
by Michael D. Davis

You don't have to know someone long to get a feeling about them. Love can grow in seconds over a few chance glances, hate does the same only in half the time. It could be the twitch of an eyebrow, the nod of a head, or just a few simple words.

I'd only known Jason for a few months, but the hate was already growing in me like a tumour. It wasn't until he said something that he couldn't take back that I knew what I had to do. It was the day that he said, "Mommy," instead of "Daddy."

Michael D. Davis was born and raised in a small town in the heart of Iowa. Having written over thirty short stories, ranging in genre from comedy to horror from flash fiction to novella he continues in his accursed pursuit of a career in the written word.

Heart Pain
by A.S. Charly

Kate took another sip of water—her second glass—while drumming her fingertips on the restaurant table.

Can't even bother to message me.

Her eyebrows rose when her husband made an entrance…but then stopped to chat with a pretty waitress.

Sure, keep me waiting.

When he finally sat with her, he smiled apologetically.

"Sorry, Honey. The traffic, you know."

"No worries."

"Could I have one of your headache pills? I got an awful one."

She nodded and handed him the package. It wasn't her problem that they didn't fit his heart medication, not her fault he never read any descriptions.

A.S. Charly loves to lose herself in fantastical worlds far away between the stars, filled with magic and wonder. She also writes and draws when her head is not stuck in the clouds. Her writing has been published in various anthologies and online publications.
Facebook: A.S.Charlydreams
Amazon: www.amazon.com/author/a.s.charly

Garrett
by Gabriella Balcom

"You're mine forever," I told Ella after we began dating. "Even if the world ends."

She said I was super intense and overdramatic, but her eyes sparkled. "Those are some of the things I love about you," she added, laughing like this was the funniest thing ever.

When I told Ella I wasn't exaggerating, she swore she'd never leave me or be unfaithful, either.

She slept with another man right after we got engaged, though.

That's why no one will ever find what's left of Ella. Of her lover, either. Like I told her in the beginning, she was *mine*.

Gabriella Balcom lives in Texas with her family, loves reading and writing, and thinks she was born with a book in her hands. She works in a mental health field, and writes fantasy, horror/thriller, romance, children's stories, and sci-fi. She likes travelling, music, good shows, photography, history, interesting tales, and animals. Gabriella says she's a sucker for a great story and loves forests, mountains, and back roads which might lead who knows where. She has a weakness for lasagne, garlic bread, tacos, cheese, and chocolate, but not necessarily in that order.
Facebook: GabriellaBalcom.lonestarauthor

Light Bulb
by Brian Rosenberger

It's dark.

Day and night blend. I calculate time by when I eat and when I fuck.

Todd was older than me, in shape, handsome. Over drinks, we exchanged small talk and later bodily fluids.

He called the following day and the day after. We were dating.

Todd suggested we try a threesome. I was young and naive.

Then I was having sex with his friends. Then complete strangers.

Todd didn't even watch, just took the cash.

A light bulb tells me it's time to eat, time to fuck.

The broken bulb was for my wrists.

Now it's for Todd.

Brian Rosenberger lives in a cellar in Marietta, GA (USA) and writes by the light of captured fireflies. He is the author of As the Worms Turns and three poetry collections. He is also a featured contributor to the Pro-Wrestling literary collection, Three-Way Dance, available from Gimmick Press.
Facebook: HeWhoSuffers

Mean Girls
by A.R. Dean

Addison is the cruellest girl at school. Her pranks go beyond simple teasing. It started with names and ended today with me being covered in canned dog food.

I weep at home and allow my rage to plan my vengeance.

My target stumbles home from a party Saturday night. I hold her ex-boyfriend's baseball bat tight in my gloved hands. I stalk her patiently until she stumbles into an alley.

I let my anger free as I beat her bloody. I drop the bat and flee. I leave her alive. Mean girls always devour their own when they are weak.

A.R. Dean is a dark and twisted soul. Dean has spent their whole life spreading fear with the tales from their head. Best known for stories that terrify and show the evilest side of human nature. So, look for Dean haunting your local cemetery or under your bed, because they're here to spread the fear. Turn off your lights and enjoy a scare. Dean is being published in Black Hare Press's Beyond and Unravel Anthologies. Keep a lookout for more stories.
Facebook: A.R. Dean Author & Ghoul

Guess My Name
by McKenzie Richardson

They thought they had seen the last of me. What fools these mortals are. We made a deal, a perfectly fair, binding deal. And that horrid miller's-daughter-turned-queen cheated.

I slink from my hollow tree home, grabbing my cap on the way out. Its colour has faded a bit to a ruddy brown. Many years have passed since I last dyed it, its fabric long overdue for a coat of fresh blood.

Then I creep through the forest toward the castle.

I was promised a child, and a child is what I shall collect. Our deal never specified dead or alive.

McKenzie Richardson lives in Milwaukee, WI. Her horror stories have been featured in various anthologies including Evil Lurks, Pandemic, and After: Undead Wars. She has also published a variety of poems and flash fiction pieces.
Facebook: mckenzielrichardson
Blog: www.craft-cycle.com

Honour
by Nicola Currie

It could not be an easy death. Not after what he did to my sister.

After we had castrated him, we took his eyes, his tongue, his fingers. I burst his ear drums with an untwisted clothes hanger.

Nothing but dark and silent pain. Father and I left him in a disfigured heap, out in the fields where wild animals would find him. I took pictures to show my sister what we had done for her.

"Monster," she called me, and fainted. I welcomed it. Her distress would scare her from further disobedience, and the wild animals that would follow.

Nicola Currie is from Cambridge, UK where she works in educational publishing. She has published poetry in literary magazines, including Mslexia and Sarasvati, and short stories in various anthologies. She has also completed her first novel, which was longlisted for the Bath Children's Novel Award. Website: writeitandweep.home.blog

The Thanksgiving Feast
by Mark Kodama

I sat across the dinner table, listening to his drivel about his promotions, his children and his philosophies. It was taking all of my willpower and self-restraint not to pick up the bowl of hot gravy and dump its entire contents on his head. I ate little of the turkey his wife cooked. It was so dry that it nearly choked me. Afterwards, on our way home from the Thanksgiving feast, my wife asked me why I could not be successful like my little brother. That night, as I lay awake, I resolved to put him out of his misery.

Mark Kodama *is a trial attorney and former newspaper reporter who lives in Washington, D.C. with his wife and two sons. He is currently working on Las Vegas Tales, a work of philosophy, sugar-coated with meter and rhyme and told through stories. His short stories and poems have been published in anthologies, on-line magazines and on-line blogs.*

Stale Mate
by Dawn DeBraal

After forty years of marriage, Karen couldn't look at Biff without dry heaving.

He was such a catch in high school. Little did she know Biff would flame out after a few years, just as she started to blossom.

He drank too much, gained thirty-seven pounds, belched the Beethoven's Fifth Symphony on command; something she used to laugh at but now detested. It seemed everything she knew about him—and that was a great deal—was no longer endearing to her. She needed to get rid of Biff before she went nuts.

Too late. While he slept, she smothered him.

Dawn DeBraal lives in rural Wisconsin with her husband Red, two rat terriers, and a cat. She has discovered that her love of telling a good story can be written. Published stories with Palm-sized press, Spillwords, Mercurial Stories, Potato Soup Journal, Edify Fiction, Zimbell House Publishing, Clarendon House Publishing, Blood Song Books, Black Hare Press, Fantasia Divinity, Cafelit, Reanimated Writers, Guilty Pleasures, Unholy Trinity, The World of Myth, Dastaan World, Vamp Cat, Runcible Spoon, Dark Christmas, Siren's Call, Iron Horse Publishing, Falling Star Magazine 2019 Pushcart Nominee.
Amazon: amazon.com/Dawn-DeBraal/e/B07STL8DLX

Zero Hour Contracts
and Bad Managers
by Kevin J. Kennedy

I hate my job. I don't mind the work. It's the people I work with. I hate incompetent managers, lazy team mates, outdated rules and policies, and the unfairness of how the hours are divided up on zero hour contracts. My boss picks his favourites. That generally means that if you have big tits and no brains, you get all the shifts. I'm going to change that though. That fat fucker has seen his last day. I got zero hours today, again. After he finishes tonight, I am going to take his life. Hopefully, the next manager will be fairer.

Kevin J. Kennedy is a horror author & editor from Scotland. He is the co-author of You Only Get One Shot & Screechers, and the publisher of several best selling anthology series; Collected Horror Shorts, 100 Word Horrors & The Horror Collection, as well as the stand alone anthology Carnival of Horror. His stories have been featured in many other notable books in the horror genre. He is an active member of the Horror Writers Association. He lives in a small town in Scotland, with his wife and his two little cats, Carlito and Ariel.
Website: www.kevinjkennedy.co.uk
Amazon: : amazon.com/Kevin-J.-Kennedy/e/B016V0NA7M

Steel Clarity
by Kimberly Rei

"Hatred is a child's emotion."

Mother's voice rang in my ears, jarring as ever. As I grew, I understood what she meant, but also how wrong she was. Hatred, wielded properly, was a refined emotion. It brought focus and clarity. It burned away all guilt and left a clean vision of the path ahead.

Blood fell from the tip of my sword. The body in front of me crumpled, inelegant. When the constable asked, Mother couldn't explain why all her suitors, every one of them a gold digger, kept vanishing after the first date.

It wasn't her story to tell.

Kimberly Rei has been writing for as long as she can remember. At five years old, her parents gifted her with a set of Children's Classics that she had no hope of reading. Yet. The potential alone sparked a love of words that has never wavered. Kim has taught writing workshops and edited novels for Authors You May Recognize. She has published several short stories and now can't stop chasing paper dragons. She currently lives in Tampa Bay, Florida with her wife and an abundance of gorgeous beaches to explore.

Happy Anniversary
by Stuart Conover

Winslow knew it was time.

Another year had passed.

He made it down the castle's spire.

Legs not quite what they used to be.

Nothing was these days.

Still, the journey had to be made.

It was their anniversary.

Down past the basement.

Through the dungeon.

Into the caves and down.

A torch his only light.

Finally, the coffin.

She lay beneath the stone slab.

Motionless.

Dead to the world.

Chained down.

Her eyes fluttered.

"Have you forgiven me my love?"

He gazed down at her eternal beauty.

Possibly for the last time.

"Never." He whispered.

Burying her once more.

Stuart Conover is a father, husband, rescue dog owner, published author, blogger, journalist, horror enthusiast, comic book geek, science fiction junkie, and IT professional. With all of that to cram in daily, we have no idea if or when he sleeps or how he gets writing done! (We suspect it has to do with having evil clones.) Stuart is a Chicago native and runs the author resource Horror Tree.

Lifting the Veil
by Paula R.C. Readman

As I lifted the lace veil from your face, I drank in your beauty. Without a care, you held on tight to the flowers that perfumed the air.

"I do," you said, making my heart soar, while all around us, our wedding party cheered.

That night, reality unveiled the truth as you muttered in your sleep, words of love that were not for me.

Fear blinded my anger as you broke my heart. In the darkness, I pushed a pillow down. You lashed out, and scattered our wedding vows among the petals from the bouquet as death tore us asunder.

***Paula R.C. Readman** learnt 'How to Write' from books which her husband purchased from eBay. After 250 purchases, he finally told her 'just to get on with the writing'. Since 2010, she's had 34 stories published.*
Blog: paulareadman1.wordpress.com

Doll Making
by A.R. Johnston

"Careful stitches, slowly… It has to be just right. It won't work otherwise."

"Are you sure about this? This will work?" She carefully pulled the red thread, pulling the needle through the doll.

"Of course it will work. Have I ever steered you wrong?" the vodoun priestess scoffed at her. "He'll feel the pain. All the pain that he has given to you will soon be replayed upon him through this doll. You just have to want it enough or it won't work."

She paused to look at the doll and to the priestess.

"He has to pay for the pain."

A.R. Johnston is a small-town girl from Nova Scotia, Canada. She is known to write mostly urban fantasy, though she goes where the muses lead her and you never know where that may be. She is a lover of coffee, good tv shows, horror flicks, and a reader of good books. She pretends to be a writer when real life doesn't get in the way. Pesky full-time job and adulting!
Facebook: arjohnstonauthor
Website: arjohnstonauthor.wordpress.com

Blood Soaked Competition
by Mark Mackey

Pickaxe.

Hatchet.

Chainsaw.

Hunting knife.

With these four dangerous toys, Amara Winsore eliminated her competition—otherwise known as her ex-boyfriend and his crew—for the student short filmmaking contest.

She hated him with a fiery passion for breaking her heart, deciding the cheerleader squad captain was the one he desired.

She killed him, and them, off one by one.

Spilled buckets of blood.

Saved him for last.

Then set up the cheerleader squad captain to take the blame; she's rotting away in prison forever.

And now Amara's dream of being the next Jenna Beckers, her filmmaker idol, is finally realised.

Mark Mackey is a speculative fiction writer who now resides in Rockford Illinois after spending an abundance of time in Chicago. The author's stories can be found in various anthologies, some charity, some not, including some belonging to Australian publisher, Black Hare Pres, and Suicide House Publishing, now known as Nocturnal Sirens Publishing, headed by Natalie Brown.

Plotting
by A.R. Johnston

He thinks he can get away with this? We've been together this long, and he thinks he can just go ahead and say such things? Simply leave his phone around so I see the texts? Really? I should just leave things and not say anything? Not bloody likely.

Why shouldn't I be happy? What won't I do to make sure that karma visits? What won't I do to make sure the threefold law comes back to him? Do unto others as you would have them do unto you. Oh my, what fun we shall have. Payback will be a bitch.

A.R. Johnston is a small-town girl from Nova Scotia, Canada. She is known to write mostly urban fantasy, though she goes where the muses lead her and you never know where that may be. She is a lover of coffee, good tv shows, horror flicks, and a reader of good books. She pretends to be a writer when real life doesn't get in the way. Pesky full-time job and adulting!
Facebook: arjohnstonauthor
Website: arjohnstonauthor.wordpress.com

Money Well Spent
by Eddie D. Moore

It took forty-two stones for Charlie to build his mailbox stand. He set the capstone in place, took three steps back, and said, "Try knocking that over."

***

Laura nearly took the curve in front of her ex-husband's house too fast, but she accelerated through the bend and eased the car off the side of the road to clip the mailbox. She realised that the new box was mounted on a stone pedestal as the capstone crashed through the windshield.

When Charlie saw his ex-wife's car in the ditch, he dialled 911 and mumbled as the phone rang, "Money well spent."

Eddie D. Moore travels hundreds of hours a year, and he fills that time by listening to audiobooks. When he isn't playing with his grandchildren, he writes his own stories. You can find a list of his publications on his blog or by visiting his Amazon Author Page. While you're there, be sure to pick up a copy of his mini-anthology Misfits & Oddities.
Website: eddiedmoore.wordpress.com
Amazon: amazon.com/author/eddiedmoore

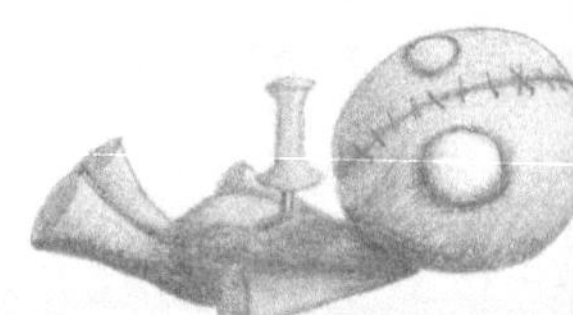

Yard Sale
by Peter J. Foote

"So, everything here is free? Even the purses and shoes, these are designer names?" one lady asks as hands reach, grab and tug to fill greedy arms with the unexpected bounty.

"Absolutely, please take everything. I've lost my wife, all her things just bring up too many upsetting memories."

"I'm sorry, dear," another lady with five purses remarks. "I hope her passing was peaceful and she didn't suffer." Hands grab a pair of designer shoes.

"Oh, she didn't die, but her suffering will only begin when she gets home and finds out that I've learned she's been cheating on me!"

Peter J. Foote is a bestselling speculative fiction writer from Nova Scotia. Outside of writing, he runs a used bookstore specialising in fantasy & sci-fi, cosplays, and alternates between red wine and coffee as the mood demands. His short stories can be found in both print and in ebook form, with his story "Sea Monkeys" winning the inaugural "Engen Books/Kit Sora, Flash Fiction/Flash Photography" contest in March of 2018. As the founder of the group "Genre Writers of Atlantic Canada", Peter believes that the writing community is stronger when it works together.
Twitter: @PeterJFoote1
Website: peterjfooteauthor.wordpress.com

Cybele's Lament
by Kate Lowe

They came in the night with their torches and judgements of heresy. They came with accusations and the might of Torquemada, that holy inquisitor. They came with their fears and their prejudice and stole away the women of the wild woods, the healers and the nurturers, we avatars of nature.

We screamed as the rack and the strappado laid waste to our bodies, their eyes on our nakedness, libidinous, revulsed. We sobbed for our sisters who had suffered so before, and we sobbed for those whose sentence lay before them.

We died with the curse of revenge on our lips.

Kate Lowe *is a writer of speculative fiction from Leicestershire, England. Her short stories have appeared in various zines, magazines and anthologies, and she has an Honourable Mention in The Best Horror of the Year Volume 4, edited by Ellen Datlow. She lives with her husband, two demanding cats and an army of bears that have far too much to say for themselves.*
Website: www.kateloweauthor.co.uk

Disgruntled
by Raven Corinn Carluk

Forty fucking years! Four decades of blood, sweat, and tears Luke had given to them, working long nights, skipping vacations. Birthdays missed, graduations unattended, grandchildren born and raised without him.

Replaced without pension, tossed aside like rubbish.

Anger seethed, low and constant. Every day tainted by thoughts of the young man who'd released him, that twist of the lips that said he didn't care.

Luke stood in the office, ready to plunge the knife into his own heart. He hadn't kept the traditions, but Maman Robicheaux had taught him many ways to punish others.

Good look releasing his vengeful spirit.

Raven Corinn Carluk writes dark fantasy, paranormal romance, and anything else that catches her interest. She's authored five novels, where she explores themes of love and acceptance. Her shorter pieces, usually from her darker side, can be found in Black Hare Press anthologies, at Detritus Online, and through Alban Lake Publishers.
Twitter: @ravencorinn
Website: www.ravencorinncarluk.com

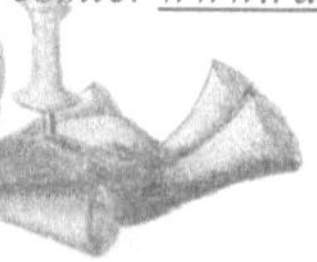

Nasty Nancy
by Amber M. Simpson

Mashed potatoes struck the lunch lady's face as the high school cafeteria erupted in its familiar chant.

"Nasty Nancy! Nasty Nancy!"

More food was flung, mac-n-cheese catching in her greasy hair, tater tots bouncing off her sagging breasts.

Nancy only grinned at the teenage faces filling the cafeteria where she'd worked – and been mocked – for three decades.

When the first loud cough broke the chanting, Nancy's smile grew wider. Soon, all the little bastards were coughing and choking, her special ingredient working its magic.

As faces turned purple and gasping breaths stopped, Nancy laughed and chanted.

"Nasty Nancy! Nasty Nancy!"

Amber M. Simpson is a dark fiction writer from Northern Kentucky with a penchant for horror and fantasy. Her work has been published in multiple anthologies, as well as online. She assists with editing for Fantasia Divinity Magazine, where she's gotten to work with many talented authors from all over the world. While she loves to create dark worlds and diverse characters, her greatest creations of all are her sons, Max and Liam, who keep her feet on the ground even while her head is in the clouds.
Website: ambermsimpson.com
Facebook: authorambermsimpson

Not Forgiven, Never Forgotten
by Rich Rurshell

Simon slashed the knife so violently through Alec's cheek, that he heard the blade strike teeth. With an equally determined swipe, he opened Alec's throat, silencing his scream.

Simon repeatedly plunged the knife into Alec's chest and face and recalled times they'd taken his lunch, or called him "Bugeye" due to his thick glasses, or "Jaws" because of his underbite. The times they had beaten him up in the bike shed after school.

They would all get what was coming to them. This was just the beginning.

The hate had always been there, Simon had just lacked confidence...

Until now.

Rich Rurshell is a short story writer from Suffolk, England. Rich writes Horror, Sci-Fi, and Fantasy, and his stories can be found in various short story anthologies and magazines. Most recently, his story "Subject: Galilee" was published in World War Four from Zombie Pirate Publishing, and "Life Choices" was published in Salty Tales from Stormy Island Publishing. When Rich is not writing stories, he likes to write and perform music.
Facebook: richrurshellauthor

Fate of an Evil Queen
by McKenzie Richardson

The stories say that they made me dance in hot iron shoes until I dropped down dead. Only half of that is true. The fact that generations of humans believe it's that easy to kill me is insulting. All of that only made me stronger.

Eating a raw heart, poisoning a princess, cold-blooded murder. That's when I used to strive to be the fairest in the land. That is far behind me now.

You think I was evil before? You just wait. You haven't seen what I am capable of now that I no longer care about being called beautiful.

McKenzie Richardson *lives in Milwaukee, WI. Her horror stories have been featured in various anthologies including Evil Lurks, Pandemic, and After: Undead Wars. She has also published a variety of poems and flash fiction pieces.*
Facebook: mckenzielrichardson
Blog: www.craft-cycle.com

Have Some Cake
by Catherine Kenwell

"You little bastards! I'll kill you!"

The neighbourhood brats had knocked on my door, run into the alleyway, and cried for help. I ran outside in my housecoat and slippers. The door locked behind me.

"I hate you!" I stammered.

The brats giggled into their hands. They pranked the neighbours regularly; I swear everyone wished them dead.

One day, I called out to them. "OK, kids, let's call a truce… Come in, have some chocolate cake."

Surprisingly, they agreed.

Cake and ice cream. Laced with antifreeze.

Crying in the alleyway? Pay no mind, it's just those brats, at it again.

Catherine Kenwell is a Barrie, Ontario, mediator and author. After 30 successful years in corporate communications, she sustained a brain injury, lost her job, and joined the circus. She writes both horror/dark fiction and inspirational non-fiction. Her works have been published in Chicken Soup for the Soul, Trembling with Fear, Siren's Call, and HellBound Books. Website: www.catherinekenwell.com

The Greatest Con Artist
by Carole de Monclin

A good con must establish confidence and the surrender of doubt.

The despicable creatures worship me. They think I love them.

A con also involves a reward, as imaginary as it's attractive.

Because they believe someday eternal happiness awaits, they forgive every nasty misfortune I inflict, while I get off on watching them struggle.

I laugh when they fight each other in the name of my different incarnations.

They even pin their hardships on the Beast, when it's really only me ruining their lives.

If I did love the gullible wretches, would I have unleashed famine, war, diseases, or taxes?

Carole de Monclin travels both the real world and imaginary ones. She's lived in France, Australia, and the USA; visited 25+ countries; and explored Mars, Ceres, and many distant planets. She writes to invite people on a journey. Her stories can be found in The Arcanist, The Deep Space Anthology, and every volume of the Dark Drabbles series.
Website: CaroledeMonclin.com
Twitter: @CaroledeMonclin

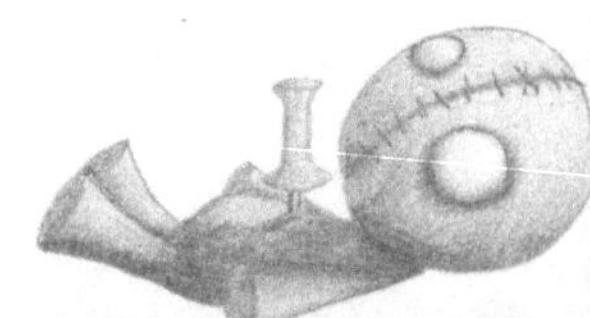

Worth It
by Wondra Vanian

There were few things Elena hated more than crowds. Very few.

When her mother died, inviting a parade of unwelcome well-wishers into Elena's life, it was hell.

She gritted her teeth as the doorbell rang yet again and another of her mother's friends appeared bearing a casserole dish. If Elena opened her mouth, she would scream.

Serves you right, she thought miserably. *Should have thought of that before…*

Her gaze fell on a framed photograph of her mother. She smiled. Nope, still worth it.

There were few things Elena hated more than crowds. Her mother had been one of them.

Wondra Vanian is an American living in the United Kingdom with her Welsh husband and their army of fur babies. A writer first, Wondra is also an avid gamer, photographer, cinephile, and blogger. She has music in her blood, sleeps with the lights on, and has been known to dance naked in the moonlight. Wondra was a multiple Top-Ten finisher in the 2017 and 2018 Preditors and Editors Reader's Poll, including the Best Author category. Her story, "Halloween Night," was named a Notable Contender for the Bristol Short Story Prize in 2015. Website: www.wondravanian.com

Circles
by Steven Lord

Urien wiped the blood from his sword with a gloved hand and surveyed the carnage around him with grim satisfaction. Finally *[how long? Why can't I remember?]* his quest for vengeance was over; Tristan lay dead at his feet.

The cur had stolen his wife from him *[no, she had loved him]*, then laughed as he cut her throat in front of him *[I remember the fear in her eyes as I raised my sword]*. Now he could rest. He sheathed his sword and strode…

…into the room and drew his sword with a roar. Finally, revenge would be his…

Steven Lord *is a debut author based in the south of England. He is currently attempting to cram writing in alongside a busy day job, with varying levels of success. While his long-term aspiration is to get a novel published, at present he would be pretty pleased with a drabble or two.*

Born to Kill
by Brianna Witte

His body shook violently against the straps. Beads of sweat pooled down his face, falling onto the chair. He begged me to let him go; to not harm him.

That was not possible. Not after how he killed my family; murdering them like wild dogs before robbing everything they owned. He would not get away with it.

The knife glistened under the florescent lighting. It was time to cut him to pieces.

"Don't worry," I said. "If you faint, I'll make sure to wake you. You liked watching my family die. I'll make sure you don't miss your own death."

*As an up and coming writer from Ontario, Canada, **Brianna Witte** has a passion for spinning tales of adventure and fantasy. She enjoys taking readers on a ride through the realm of fiction by weaving magical and mystical stories that materialise from her wildly creative dreams and vivid imagination. To date she has had a number of short stories and drabbles published, as well as her short story, 'The Hunt' commended for the 2019 Author of Tomorrow award. She also had a novel, Witches and Vampires, published in December 2019.*
Facebook: BriannaWitteAuthor
Instagram: briannawitteauthor

End of a Rivalry
by Radar DeBoard

John sat by the fireplace, reminiscing on his long rivalry with Paul. He remembered that it started sometime during high school.

They always tried to outdo each other both academically and physically. They had kept it going for more than twenty years. Two decades of sneaky tricks and backstabbing to get the upper hand.

John couldn't place the exact moment where it crossed from a friendly rivalry into pure hatred. All John knew was that he had been the one to make the final move. He looked up at Paul's mounted head on the mantelpiece. The perfect place for it.

Radar DeBoard is a horror movie and novel enthusiast who resides in the small town of Goddard, Kansas. He occasionally dabbles in writing, and enjoys to make dark tales for people to enjoy. He has had drabbles and short stories published in various electronic magazines and anthologies.
Facebook: WriterRadarDeBoard

Delicacy
by Cassandra Angler

"You're such a waste of space. Of air. Of flesh." She struggles against her restraints, screams muffled by tape. "Go ahead and struggle. I like a challenge." I tighten the restraints, her fingers swollen and purple. Blood sprays as I bite the tip of her finger off. She screams again as I chew. I lick the blood from my lips. "I can taste the hatred in your blood." She weeps, tears staining her dirty cheeks. I can't help but laugh, her eyes round and large. "You won't be missed." I slash her throat. Her lifeless eyes gaze up at me.

Cassandra Angler is a married mother of four who lives in the State of Ohio in the USA. When she isn't busy caring for her family, Cassandra works on her upcoming novel due out in November of 2020 titled Contaminated. Cassandra has three short story publications as well as several flash fiction and drabble publications.

Sauce
by Kimberly Rei

Smiling, she set a plate before me.

I raised my fork, senses flaring at the first bite of pasta. Her skill with cuisine was known, but she had outdone herself. If I became dizzy with joy, what of it? This woman and this meal would make anyone heady. My tongue convulsed in delight.

Pleasure became panic as my mouth went numb.

There were rumours of unusual deaths; half-eaten pastries and lifeless bodies. I'd always scoffed. Talk was cheap.

Her ruby lips twisted. There was a glint in her gaze. A loathing. Her voice slid around me. Liquid. Casual. "Who's Daphne?"

Kimberly Rei has been writing for as long as she can remember. At five years old, her parents gifted her with a set of Children's Classics that she had no hope of reading. Yet. The potential alone sparked a love of words that has never wavered. Kim has taught writing workshops and edited novels for Authors You May Recognize. She has published several short stories and now can't stop chasing paper dragons. She currently lives in Tampa Bay, Florida with her wife and an abundance of gorgeous beaches to explore.

The Last Word
by Glenn R. Wilson

I love irony.

I laugh as I push the tube into your vein. To think that a few months ago I held you in my arms. Now, I watch as your blood runs out and I replace it with another fluid.

It's your fault, you know. You told me I'd never touch you again when you left me for that man. The one who's arrested for poisoning you. He'll fry, alright—I made sure of that by planting evidence.

Now, I smile at your lovely face as I caress your cold body.

Most fun I've ever had as a mortician.

Glenn R. Wilson has come full circle. Making a point to mature, like fine wine, before diving head-first into his long list of writing projects, he's approaching them with a plan. That strategy is to build with one brick at a time. He's accumulated a few bricks already and is adding more. Over time, with persistence and determination, he'll have a home. But for now, a solid foundation is the goal. Please, enjoy the process with him.

The Circle
by Ximena Escobar

"I wrote a story about you," I said.

"Really?" Lucy's conceited gaze travelled across 'the circle', but I saw her mockery too.

"Amazing!" said Laura, unable to disguise her sarcasm.

Lucy laughed behind her smile, avoiding the looks happening between the others—aware that my eyes were fixed on her.

"What's it about?" asked Laura.

"It's quite a dark, ominous piece…"

They all exploded in laughter—it had to be dark, coming from me.

"What's wrong?" I asked. "Can't any of you breathe?" (They were all turning purple but only I was laughing.) "You'll see it has a happy ending…"

Ximena Escobar is writing stories and poetry. Originally from Chile, she is the author of a translation into Spanish of the Broadway Musical "The Wizard of Oz", and of an original adaptation of the same, "Navidad en Oz", both produced in her home country. Since 2018 she has published several short stories in various anthologies and online platforms, and is now slowly working on her own collection. Ximena has a degree in Arts & Communication Science and lives in Nottingham with her family.
Facebook: Ximenautora
Twitter: @laximenin

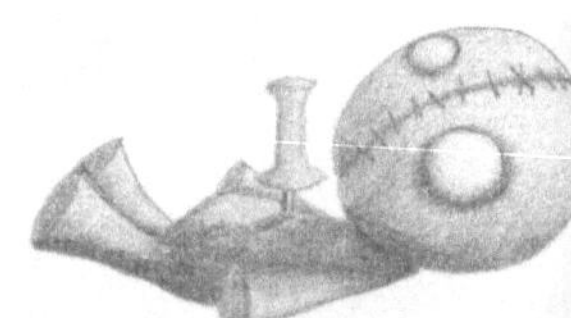

Devolution of Love
by N.M. Brown

Our first date came, and it was love at first sight.

Our second date came, I knew you were just right.

When our third date arrived, you'd already been inside.

On our fourth date, you begged me to be your one and only; always there for the ride.

By the time I got pregnant, you were nowhere in sight

The memories I still have from you, each one is from a fight.

By the time you finally hit me, there was no love left to give

By the time they find your body, you'll have no more life to live.

*Since **N.M. Brown** made her first post to a popular Internet forum, she's taken the horror community by storm. Her ability to create, terrify, and drive home her stories is insurmountable. N.M. Brown's published works can be found in multiple anthologies for all to read, but be forewarned, if you do... you may want to call your therapist after, her stories are terrifying, disturbing and devilishly unsettling. She is not only a fright visually, but also has a creepy tentacle in horror podcasting as well. Sinister Sweetheart writes, voice acts and is the media director of the Scarecrow Tales podcast.*
Website: Sinistersweetheart.wixsite.com/sinistersweetheart
Facebook: NMBrownStories

Venom
by Joachim Heijndermans

Smile. Put on a happy face when the boss is here. Pretend the sight of him doesn't make me retch, or that when he touches me, I want to peel the skin from my bones.

The others he pimps me out to I can handle. Some are gentle, and slip me some cash on the side, which I've saved up for some new teeth. Special teeth.

Boss likes them, saying it makes my mouth look sexy. Makes me use it, too. Tells me to be careful with them. Doesn't notice the retractable tips laced in venom until it's too late.

Joachim Heijndermans writes, draws, and paints nearly every waking hour. Originally from the Netherlands, he's been all over the world, boring people by spouting random trivia. His work has been featured in a number of anthologies and publications, such as Mad Scientist Journal, Asymmetry Fiction, Hinnom Magazine, Ahoy Comics's Edgar Allan Poe's Snifter of Terror, Metaphorosis and The Gallery of Curiosities, and he's currently in the midst of completing his first children's book.
Website: www.joachimheijndermans.com
Twitter: @jheijndermans

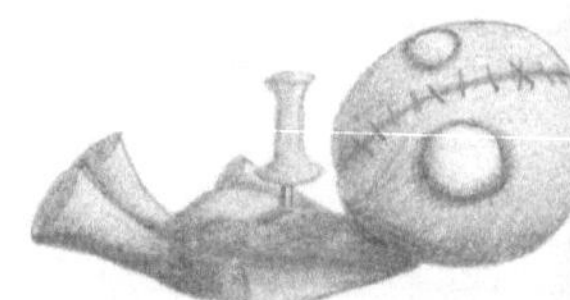

The Borrower
by Kathleen Halecki

Staring in horror, she surveyed the book. The cover was torn, the corners were dog-eared, and the pages were oddly yellowed. He shrugged at her expression.

"Is this how you return a book?"

"The coffee spilled."

She pressed her lips together grimly, "Should we be drinking coffee around books?" She could feel the anger welling up within her. Too much sloppiness these days, she thought.

He shrugged again, "It is just a book."

She smiled brightly, reached into the desk and felt for the letter-opener. With a quick movement, she stabbed him in the eye.

"No more books for you."

Kathleen Halecki possesses a B.A. and M.A. in history, and a doctoral degree in interdisciplinary studies. Although born in New York, she currently resides in a seventeenth century home in New England. Her work can be found in The Copperfield Review; Shadows in Salem: Wicked Tales from the Witch City; One Night in Salem; Midnight Rising: A Collection of Paranormal Tales; From a Cat's View Volume II, and Shadow of Pendle. She has also drabbled before in Curses and Cauldrons and Forest of Fear.

Arachnids
by Vonnie Winslow Crist

Dayton Thomas grinned while spraying the black widow infestation with pesticide. He'd always enjoyed killing insects and arachnids. He'd been destined to found DT's Pest Control since childhood.

After he'd eliminated the spiders, the homeowner generously tipped him.

A smiling DT went home and relaxed on his porch on a Mexican chair he'd picked up at a secondhand store. He felt a pinch, looked at his hand, and saw a *Loxosceles tenochtitlan*.

"No!" he screamed before killing the spider.

Well-versed in arachnology, Dayton knew an ever-expanding lesion of dead flesh would soon develop.

"Apparently, the hate is mutual," he said.

Vonnie Winslow Crist is author of The Enchanted Dagger, Owl Light, The Greener Forest, Murder on Marawa Prime, and other award-winning books. Her fiction is included in "Amazing Stories," "Cast of Wonders," "Outposts of Beyond," Killing It Softly 2, Defending the Future - Dogs of War, Midnight Masquerade, Chaos of Hard Clay, and elsewhere. A cloverhand who has found so many four-leafed clovers she keeps them in jars, Vonnie strives to celebrate the power of myth in her writing.
Website: www.vonniewinslowcrist.com

Ironic
by Ximena Escobar

to your stupid tic,

to your foolish text,

to your wicked tongue,

to your flaccid sex,

to your mother's grin,

to your mocking laugh,

to the soup on your chin,

to your female staff,

to the date you forgot,

to the hand you didn't give,

to the pounds you wish I lost,

to the spite you can't forgive,

to your smoke up my nose,

to the point that

eludes you: thank you!

'cause I owe to all this,

that I don't mince my words,

don't beat around the bush

but, always

find my "love" for you,

when regret haunts me.

Ximena Escobar is writing stories and poetry. Originally from Chile, she is the author of a translation into Spanish of the Broadway Musical "The Wizard of Oz", and of an original adaptation of the same, "Navidad en Oz", both produced in her home country. Since 2018 she has published several short stories in various anthologies and online platforms, and is now slowly working on her own collection. Ximena has a degree in Arts & Communication Science and lives in Nottingham with her family.
Facebook: _Ximenautora_
Twitter: _@laximenin_

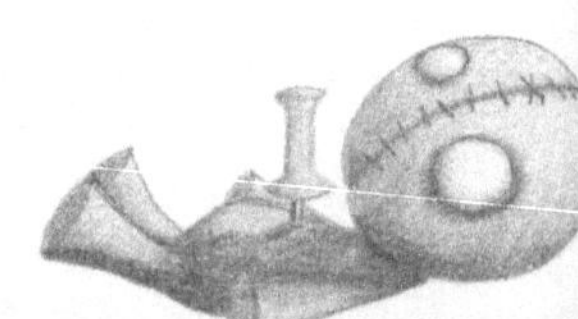

Cyber-Vengeance
by Jo Mularczyk

"Hi Grace, I know this is awkward, but I really need your help."

Grace sat in stunned silence at the other end of the phone, but he ploughed on unperturbed. "My computer has a virus and the tech guys need to wipe my hard drive."

"Nick when you broke up with me, we stopped sharing more than just a bed. The free tech advice dried up too!"

"I realise that Grace. I'm just asking if you've done a recent backup. I can't risk losing everything. It would ruin me."

Without the slightest pang of guilt, she smoothly lied, "Sure did."

Jo Mularczyk's stories and poems appear in magazines and anthologies including - The School Magazine's Blast Off and Touchdown; Zinewest 2017, 2018, 2019; Short and Twisted 2017; Open House 2 and 3; Short Tales 4 and 5; Christmas Tales 4; Wonderment; an upcoming Bloomsbury UK book of poems for children; fourW thirty; and several upcoming publications. Jo mentors gifted and talented students' writing groups, runs junior writing workshops and is a co-author with the student literacy program, Littlescribe. Through Littlescribe Jo provides writing tips and story starters for students to complete as co-authors. Jo lives in Australia with her husband and three children.
Website: www.jomularczyk.com
Facebook: jo.mularczyk.author

Roofer
by David Bowmore

Politicians—I fuckin' hate 'em.

Ya' know we don't get pensioned till we're sixty-seven now. Easy for them to say on eighty grand a year. There ain't one o' them deserves one fuckin' penny. I'd like to see them up a roof when they're sixty-seven years old with my knees.

I've had it with Brexit and Euro MPs.

An' I got a parking ticket yesterday, too. Fuckin' council, robbin' bastards.

Wankers—I'd shoot 'em all.

Anyway, Guv, new gutter an' down-pipe to rear o' the house; hundred an' fifty quid all in.

I'll do it next Wednesday, if ya like.

David Bowmore *has lived here, there and everywhere, but now lives in Yorkshire with his wonderful wife and a small white poodle. He has worn many hats in his time; head chef, teacher and landscape gardener. His first collection of short stories 'The Magic of Deben Market' is available from Clarendon House.*
Website: davidbowmore.co.uk
Facebook: davidbowmoreauthor

Hunter
by A.R. Dean

They raised me to have a dark heart. To love my own kind in the secluded commune far from the lesser beings outside.

At fifteen, I am now a man. My father is taking me hunting. The bright city lights make me long for our desert home.

We wait in the alleys for a disgusting different to come by. Father holds it while I stab.

"We need more," he whispers.

In the crowded city, it doesn't take long. We load them in the truck.

He ruffles my hair with his bloody hand, "Tonight we feast on our enemies like kings."

A.R. Dean is a dark and twisted soul. Dean has spent their whole life spreading fear with the tales from their head. Best known for stories that terrify and show the evilest side of human nature. So, look for Dean haunting your local cemetery or under your bed, because they're here to spread the fear. Turn off your lights and enjoy a scare. Dean is being published in Black Hare Press's Beyond and Unravel Anthologies. Keep a lookout for more stories.
Facebook: A.R. Dean Author & Ghoul

Teach Me
by J.W. Garrett

Kelly slid into the desk. The fifth grade classroom hadn't changed.

"Can I help you? You're too old for my class. Not that I would mind."

"You don't remember?" She watched his mind churning. "Let me help, Mr. Wilson."

Kelly lifted two fingers; all the desks but hers rose into the air. He gulped, scooting toward the door.

"You… I was protecting the class."

"By beating me in front of my peers…"

"You couldn't act out if you were subdued."

"I can now." Flicking her wrist, Kelly levitated him then apparated away. As he crashed, she counted each bone breaking.

J.W. Garrett has been writing in one form or another since she was a teenager. She currently lives in Florida with her family but loves the mountains of Virginia where she was born. Her writings include YA fantasy as well as short stories. Since completing Remeon's Quest-Earth Year 1930, the prequel in her YA fantasy series, Realms of Chaos, she has been hard at work on the next in the series, scheduled to release August 2020. When she's not hanging out with her characters, her favourite activities are reading, running and spending time with family.
Website: www.jwgarrett.com
BHC Press: www.bhcpress.com/Author_JW_Garrett.html

I Hate That Rat
by D.M. Burdett

The rat scuttles across the cellar floor.

I rise from the soiled mattress, but the rattle of chains startles it into a scurry. It seems to skip gleefully, wide smile on its furry fucking face.

My dreams are filled with the taste of its juicy body—a constant phantom memory—but the rodent toys with me.

I look at the crimson plash that spreads from beneath my captor's head; those rickety stairs are both my saviour and my downfall—no-one comes when I scream. Not even him.

The rat, atop the greying face, pauses wet gnawing to watch my tears.

D.M. Burdett initially roamed as an army brat, but now lives in Australia where she spends her days avoiding drop bears and killer spiders. She has published a Sci-Fi series, has short stories in various anthologies, and has published two children's series. She is currently working on the first book in a dystopian series.
Website: www.dmburdett.com
Facebook: DMBurdett

One Night in the Lumber Camp
by McKenzie Richardson

Vines silently slithered closer to the camp, camouflaged as snakes in the underbrush by the dim light of the stars overhead. Their tendrils outstretched, pulled on by the murderous promise of pathways down throats to take up residence in stomachs and chest cavities. At the first building, a few twisted their way under the door, unlatching it for the others. They moved into the room, in search of their soon-to-be victims. The last vine curled around a lone axe left abandoned at the door, dragging it in its wake.

The humans cut down the trees. But these trees cut back.

McKenzie Richardson lives in Milwaukee, WI. Her horror stories have been featured in various anthologies including Evil Lurks, Pandemic, and After: Undead Wars. She has also published a variety of poems and flash fiction pieces.
Facebook: mckenzielrichardson
Blog: www.craft-cycle.com

The Doll
by Lesley Drane

I bought the doll in a charity shop. Made of cloth with blue buttons for eyes, yellow wool for hair; dressed in dungarees. I already had the pins.

I stuck a pin in the doll's arm and waited.

"Ow!"

Another pin, this time in the foot.

"Arrgh!"

This is so much fun! I picked up another pin and stuck in her button eye.

Silence.

Oh, no response? I listened at the kitchen door, still silence.

I jabbed a pin into the doll's heart.

"Uuuuhhhh."

I peeked around the kitchen door, yes! The wife is dead!

Not a mark in sight.

Lesley Drane is a widow, and lives with her two year old Cavalier King Charles spaniel, Stephanie. Lesley enjoys to write stories about the supernatural and murder mysteries. Lesley also makes book sculptures using preloved books.

The Last Supper
by Shelly Jarvis

He thinks I don't know. He thinks me a fool. But I've read the signs and I know what must be done.

I prepare his favourite meal, setting the table as he walks in the door. I smile, but inwardly I'm cursing the very sight of him. He wreaks of her sickly-sweet perfume and I hold my breath to avoid breathing her in.

As he slices into his dinner, I faintly wonder if she loves him. What will it do to her? Will she speak at his funeral? I won't. I'll be long gone, and my heart will be free.

Shelly Jarvis is a speculative fiction author from West Virginia, US. She found a life-long love of sci-fi and fantasy in the 3rd grade when she found Madeleine L'Engle's "A Wrinkle in Time." Shelly is an avid reader, a Whovian, the ideal viewer of dog rescue videos, and undoubtedly Ravenclaw. She currently has three YA sci-fi books available for purchase on Amazon. Website: www.ShellyJarvis.com

Propolis
by Maura Yzmore

Old queen Bud-Ihm, spry on six legs yet almost blind in the ocelli, watches her home world vanish on the ship's honeycomb screen.

An invasive species poisoned the fields and left Bud-Ihm's offspring hungry, ravaged by mites, weaker and sicker with each generation. So she gathered her children, promising fragrant meadows under a different sun.

Bud-Ihm's compound eyes darken. There are no fragrant meadows under a different sun. Her children will all die on this journey. But, without Bud-Ihm's kin, the flora that sustains the invaders will perish, and those who destroyed her world will starve. Bud-Ihm feels no remorse.

Maura Yzmore is a writer and science professor based in the American Midwest. Some of her darker fare can be found in The Molotov Cocktail, Aphotic Realm, Coffin Bell, and elsewhere. Website: maurayzmore.com
Twitter: @MauraYzmore

Dig Two Graves
by Aaron Channel

The workers thought it was odd to dig a well when the home was already connected to city water, but money answers questions better than any excuse.

His youth spent in construction was helpful for the finishing touches.

His rotten trash and bathwater had to be dumped somewhere, anyway.

Some sins are too great to be forgiven, or even repaid with a quick death.

Every year on his wife's birthday, he'd remove the stone cover and listen for screams, just to be sure.

If there was any justice, the monster would live for as long as his wife was dead.

Aaron Channel is a family man, cook, and computer nerd. His work appears in the anthologies "Curses & Cauldrons" and "Organic Ink Volume One."

Shattered Trust
by Lesley Drane

I saw them. Anger surged within me, and I quietly seethed. My best friend and my husband—how dare they!

I trusted them, I loved them both, but this betrayal… I turned away. I had to do something, but what? Did they think I wouldn't find out? I walked away, towards a bench; it had an inscribed plate screwed to it.

"For my beloved husband David," it read. I wanted to cry for the loss, for the hopes and dreams dashed by death.

I had already killed them once. My David—even as a bloody ghost, he couldn't be faithful!

Lesley Drane *is a widow, and lives with her two year old Cavalier King Charles spaniel, Stephanie. Lesley enjoys to write stories about the supernatural and murder mysteries. Lesley also makes book sculptures using preloved books.*

In Sight
by Jeff Slade

His target in sight, Ethan tensed. He gritted his teeth, hatred seething through his veins.

You've got this, he told himself. *You can do this.*

The man deserved to die. He'd made his life a living hell.

Ethan put the pistol down, wiped sweat off his hands, picked it back up.

Alright, he thought, staring ahead. *Time to meet your maker.*

He lifted his firearm before he could talk himself out of it, aimed for the head. The trigger's tension screamed for release. Ethan obliged.

With a bang, he slumped over, falling to the floor along with the mirror's reflection.

Jeff Slade resides in Salmon Cove, Newfoundland and Labrador, with his wife and two cats. He enjoys reading, writing, and making horrible puns, not necessarily in that order. You can find other short stories by him in Chillers From The Rock, Dystopia From The Rock, and Flights From The Rock, published by Engen Books.

The Blessed Dead
by Matthew M. Montelione

I stirred upon hearing familiar words spoken by a clumsy tongue. What was happening? I was in a deep slumber; an eternal paradise where I walked through the halls of the ancient gods in peace and joy.

I was slowly drawn back into the cold dark world, ripped from the safety of Anubis. I felt pain again. My stiff limbs ached, my eyes forced open by the foolish outlander who stood before me in horror.

Disturber of the blessed dead! I despised him for bringing me back. I smiled as my decayed hand gripped the villain's neck until it snapped.

***Matthew M. Montelione** is a horror writer and American Revolution historian born and raised on Long Island in New York. His work has been published in many titles, including MONSTERS: A Horror Microfiction Anthology, Quoth the Raven: A Contemporary Reimagining of the Works of Edgar Allan Poe, Thuggish Itch: Devilish, WHAT IF?: History Rewritten, Long Island History Journal, and Journal of the American Revolution. Matthew lives with his wife in New York. Website: maybeevils.com*
Facebook: maybeevils

Patience
by Stephen Christie

It's sad how much hate can breed from love. Anyone who has been in love knows that all emotions intensify, but only some of us know how strong hatred can become.

I married Marilyn in 1981. Even at the age of twenty, I knew she was the one. I truly loved her. That fire in her eyes.

How I wept as I watched that light fade away, as my hands tightened around her throat. I never stopped loving her.

My hate was not for Marilyn, but for her lover. So, I hurt him in the worst way I knew how.

*A lifelong bookworm, cinephile, and wine connoisseur, **Stephen Christie** has decided to lay off the drink, and try his hand at a little creative writing of his own. A fan of Horror, Science Fiction, Military Fiction, and Historical Fiction, he hopes his years of enjoying a collection of great books will aid him in this new endeavour.*

Newer Model
by Dawn DeBraal

He bragged about the affair. The woman was younger and prettier. Todd told Tanya intimate details that burned her ears and broke her heart. He came by to pick up their dog, Skippy. Todd never even liked Skippy. He took him only to be cruel to her.

"After twelve years of marriage, I'm trading you in for a newer model," Todd joked, laughing cruelly.

Tanya saw red everywhere. It was Todd's blood all over the kitchen. She had to pull him off. She hadn't told Todd about the new dog she bought today, or the dog's hatred of laughing men.

Dawn DeBraal lives in rural Wisconsin with her husband Red, two rat terriers, and a cat. She has discovered that her love of telling a good story can be written. Published stories with Palm-sized press, Spillwords, Mercurial Stories, Potato Soup Journal, Edify Fiction, Zimbell House Publishing, Clarendon House Publishing, Blood Song Books, Black Hare Press, Fantasia Divinity, Cafelit, Reanimated Writers, Guilty Pleasures, Unholy Trinity, The World of Myth, Dastaan World, Vamp Cat, Runcible Spoon, Dark Christmas, Siren's Call, Iron Horse Publishing, Falling Star Magazine 2019 Pushcart Nominee.
Amazon: amazon.com/Dawn-DeBraal/e/B07STL8DLX

Karma
by A.R. Johnston

It burned within her chest brightly. So much so that she felt it might burst from within her. Who knew that someone could feel such hatred toward a person, that it felt this way? It was a physical pain, making it hurt to breathe.

How could anyone feel like this, day in and day out? How was this any way to live? It had to stop. It would stop if she had anything to do with it. Refusing to be a victim anymore. Karma would come back to haunt whoever had done this to her.

It would not be pretty.

A.R. Johnston is a small-town girl from Nova Scotia, Canada. She is known to write mostly urban fantasy, though she goes where the muses lead her and you never know where that may be. She is a lover of coffee, good tv shows, horror flicks, and a reader of good books. She pretends to be a writer when real life doesn't get in the way. Pesky full-time job and adulting!
Facebook: arjohnstonauthor
Website: arjohnstonauthor.wordpress.com

Bloodied Lips
by Hari Navarro

I look at you and I hate the way your breasts wrench at the buttons of your blouse.

I look at you and I hate the way your groin swells as you strut and flex in the sand.

I look at you and I hate the way your eyes dart away when they pass through my gaze.

You look at me and you hate the way they plead when you stab.

You look at me and you hate the way bodies stink when they bloat.

You look at me and you hate how bitter my flesh tastes at your lips.

Hari Navarro has, for many years now, been locked in his neighbours cellar. He survives due to an intravenous feed of puréed extreme horror and Absinthe infused sticky-spiced unicorn wings. His anguished cries for help can be found via 365 Tomorrows, Breachzine, AntipodeanSF, Horror Without Borders, Black Hare Press and HellBound books. Hari was the Winner of the Australasian Horror Writers' Association [AHWA] Flash Fiction Award 2018 and has, also, succeeded in being a New Zealander who now lives in Northern Italy with no cats.
Amazon: amazon.com/Hari-Navarro
Tumblr: harinavarro.tumblr.com

Justice for Danny
by A.R. Dean

He was my only son. At five he disappeared from my yard, his body found in a creek two days later. What that man did to my child, I will never forgive.

He walked free today. My child's murderer returns to fresh air because of some misplaced evidence. The brute smiled and winked as he passed me by.

There is no smile now. Only fear. I will do everything to him that he did to my son, and more. My hand tingles with anticipation as I begin. The smell of his flesh roasting under a lit cigarette makes me giddy.

A.R. Dean is a dark and twisted soul. Dean has spent their whole life spreading fear with the tales from their head. Best known for stories that terrify and show the evilest side of human nature. So, look for Dean haunting your local cemetery or under your bed, because they're here to spread the fear. Turn off your lights and enjoy a scare. Dean is being published in Black Hare Press's Beyond and Unravel Anthologies. Keep a lookout for more stories.
Facebook: A.R. Dean Author & Ghoul

Justified
by Chris Bannor

"I was always taught to take the compliment. Smile. Wave. Act like some asshole wasn't judging my self-worth based on my body. Let's be honest," she said with a smirk. "They sure as hell weren't catcalling my sparking personality. The shits weren't even close enough to see my face, let alone get to know who I was."

Every member of her audience whimpered as she pulled a knife from the bag at her feet.

"It was bad enough back then. But let me explain what's going to happen to you boys, now that you started that shit with my daughter."

Chris Bannor is a science fiction and fantasy writer who lives in Southern California. Chris learned her love of genre stories from her mother at an early age and has never veered far from that path. She also enjoys musical theater and road trips with her family but is a general homebody otherwise.
Facebook: chrisbannorauthor
Website: ChrisBannor.com

Death to the Devil
by A.R. Dean

He has lain beside me every night for fourteen years. My once passionate love is now a burning hate.

His snores and beer breath haunt my dreams. How could I have ever wanted one such as he?

Drinking and beatings fill my life. I am a prisoner in my own home. I see no way out. There is no escape from the devil that sleeps beside me.

Tonight, I can no longer contain the darkness he has done to my tender heart. He is surprised as I bring the axe down upon his chest. I smile, covered in his blood.

A.R. Dean is a dark and twisted soul. Dean has spent their whole life spreading fear with the tales from their head. Best known for stories that terrify and show the evilest side of human nature. So, look for Dean haunting your local cemetery or under your bed, because they're here to spread the fear. Turn off your lights and enjoy a scare. Dean is being published in Black Hare Press's Beyond and Unravel Anthologies. Keep a lookout for more stories.
Facebook: <u>A.R. Dean Author & Ghoul</u>

The Plastic Anarchist
by Tristan Drue Rogers

Gib lived as any liberal arts student with two wealthy parents could, by burning bridges with the corporate masters of University, instigating expulsion.

His girlfriend loved his rebellions, suggesting that he put the effort that upset his father into an art show. Gib freefell into the perfect way for paying daddy back for making Gib split the tuition difference.

When opening night started, Gib's parents were led by his girlfriend to his exhibit.

The horrified look on their faces were the last images Gib saw as he hung from the ceiling, drowning in a plastic bag filled with purified water.

Tristan Drue Rogers has had his writing and poetry featured in literary magazines (such as Vamp Cat, Genre: Urban Arts, Weird Mask, and more), and horror anthologies (such as 100 Word Horrors Book 3 & 4 and Twenty Twenty). Tristan lives with his lovely wife Sarah and their son Rhett in Texas.
Website: www.tristandrue.wordpress.com
Twitter: @RogersDrue

Marinated
by Raven Corinn Carluk

Jazmine always knew the moment they fell in love with her. It was a certain piquant taste to their kisses, undefinable, but one she'd become familiar with.

That peculiar spice meant all her work had paid off. Beyond mere flirting, long past simple sex, and deep into the passions of love. Jazmine's pheromones always started the connection, but only after steeping in them would someone's heart open to the succubus.

She'd learned to savour the hunt, to enjoy the delicacy of their full emotions. A perfect meal took time to prepare, to get just right.

Rebeccah finally tasted like love.

Raven Corinn Carluk writes dark fantasy, paranormal romance, and anything else that catches her interest. She's authored five novels, where she explores themes of love and acceptance. Her shorter pieces, usually from her darker side, can be found in Black Hare Press anthologies, at Detritus Online, and through Alban Lake Publishers.
Twitter: @ravencorinn
Website: www.ravencorinncarluk.com

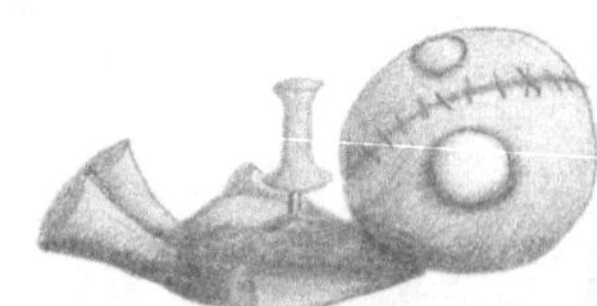

Combustible Loathing
by Terry Miller

Seeing Natalie with Bruce burned Frank's ass. As if it wasn't enough that she cheated on him with the Cro-Mag, she had to flaunt it everywhere she knew he'd be. Typical. He guessed the best revenge is to just have fun himself.

He had another shot, a nice burn going down. *That stupid bitch! What fucking nerve!* Another shot. Another. *There's nothing like downing some more trusty anger fuel,* he thought to himself. By now, his blood was boiling, quite literally. Frank poured the sweat, the liquor streaming from his pores. His body ignited in flames, burning to mere ash.

*Terry Miller lives in Portsmouth, Ohio. His work has been featured in Sanitarium Magazine, Devolution Z, Jitter, Rhysling Anthology 2017, Poetry Quarterly, Sirens Call Ezine, The Horror Tree's Trembling With Fear, SpillWords, Organic Ink Vol. I, Curses & Cauldrons Anthology from Blood Song Books, Forest of Fear from Blood Song Books, the Dark Drabble Anthology Series from Black Hare Press, 100 Word Zombie Bites from Reanimated Writers Press, Scary Snippets, Guilty Pleasures & Other Dark Delights, 100 Word Horrors 3, and O Unholy Night In Deathlehem from Grinning Skull Press.
Facebook: tmiller2015
Amazon: amazon.com/author/millerterryl*

Wipe Out
by Dawn DeBraal

Darla loved Jimmy, but his family, was another subject. From day one, they tried to drive a wedge between Darla and her true love. Jimmy stood by and watched the fighting, never siding with either side. Darla was hurt by him.

"Why don't you defend me, I'm your girlfriend?" Jimmy shrugged his shoulders.

"It's my Ma, what can I do?" Infuriated, Darla decided she would shut Jimmy's family up once and for all. He dumped her after the funeral.

"I never loved you, I just knew you could get the job done." Darla made sure she shut Jimmy up too.

Dawn DeBraal lives in rural Wisconsin with her husband Red, two rat terriers, and a cat. She has discovered that her love of telling a good story can be written. Published stories with Palm-sized press, Spillwords, Mercurial Stories, Potato Soup Journal, Edify Fiction, Zimbell House Publishing, Clarendon House Publishing, Blood Song Books, Black Hare Press, Fantasia Divinity, Cafelit, Reanimated Writers, Guilty Pleasures, Unholy Trinity, The World of Myth, Dastaan World, Vamp Cat, Runcible Spoon, Dark Christmas, Siren's Call, Iron Horse Publishing, Falling Star Magazine 2019 Pushcart Nominee.
Amazon: *amazon.com/Dawn-DeBraal/e/B07STL8DLX*

Witch Burning
by Paula R.C. Readman

A black feather floated to the ground as the crows took flight.

I saw it as a sign that he was no longer mine. Hadn't the witch forewarned me?

She called herself my *friend* as she turned the card, and said, "It's written, and cannot be undone."

I didn't believe in such things, not when we have the internet.

"I love him," she said.

Like that made all the difference.

Betrayal comes too easily to the lips of liars.

The black smoke rose as I poked the fire around her feet and reminded myself that they burnt witches long ago.

Paula R.C. Readman learnt 'How to Write' from books which her husband purchased from eBay. After 250 purchases, he finally told her 'just to get on with the writing'. Since 2010, she's had 34 stories published.
Blog: paulareadman1.wordpress.com

Baking with Magic
by A.R. Johnston

"Dear, sweet sister, what shall I bake? A cake too sweet, a biscuit too cheap. A pie it shall be. Made with all my love to hate. Will that be too good for him, d'ya think?" she sang out, flitting around the kitchen.

Her sister sat at the table, sipping her tea, chuckling and shaking her head.

"Now you're rhyming? You really have it in for this guy, don't you?"

"Rhyming makes the magic stick. The dessert will be his downfall, it will do just the trick." She brandished a wooden mixing spoon.

"So shall it be, my sister dear."

A.R. Johnston is a small-town girl from Nova Scotia, Canada. She is known to write mostly urban fantasy, though she goes where the muses lead her and you never know where that may be. She is a lover of coffee, good tv shows, horror flicks, and a reader of good books. She pretends to be a writer when real life doesn't get in the way. Pesky full-time job and adulting!
Facebook: arjohnstonauthor
Website: arjohnstonauthor.wordpress.com

HATE

ACKNOWLEDGEMENTS

Huge thanks to all the authors who have contributed to HATE, the eighth book in the Dark Drabbles series and our sixteenth publication.

We saw a whole new batch of emerging writers submit to this anthology—it was a popular theme—and you all nailed it. So, well done.

We are lucky to be surrounded by great authors who are willing to submit to our anthologies, and we'll continue to showcase their work for as long as they allow us.

As always, a very special *thank you* to you, our loyal and dedicated readers, who continue to support our work.

www.blackharepress.com

Stories of new worlds, new creatures, alien colonisation, humanity's new home, space accidents, alien snackcidents, evil planets, military mashups, alien autopsies, and much, much more.

Beatific angels, holy wars, kitty saviours, epic battles between good and evil, devils and demons, fallen angels and many more tantalising tiny tales.

Wendigos, vampires, things that go bump in the night or hide under the bed, witches, demons, upirs, kelpies, toad people, zombies, sirens and hundreds of other tiny terrifying tales.

Micro myths of the paranormal; poltergeists, spirit boards, ghosts and ghouls, avenging apparitions and horrifying hauntings.

Murder mysteries, criminal chronicles, whodunnits, revenge, suspicion, mayhem, intrigue, and lots more.

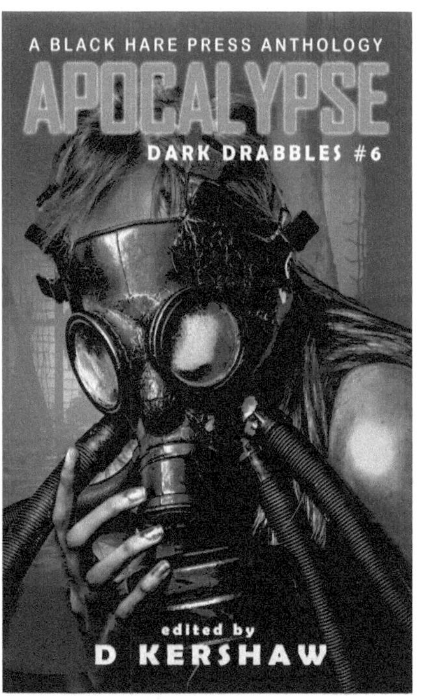

A post-apocalyptic adventure of tiny proportions. Venture into the unknown, into a time when society has broken down and every man, woman and child (and the odd monster or alien) must fight for themselves.

Twisted tales of love in tiny portions.

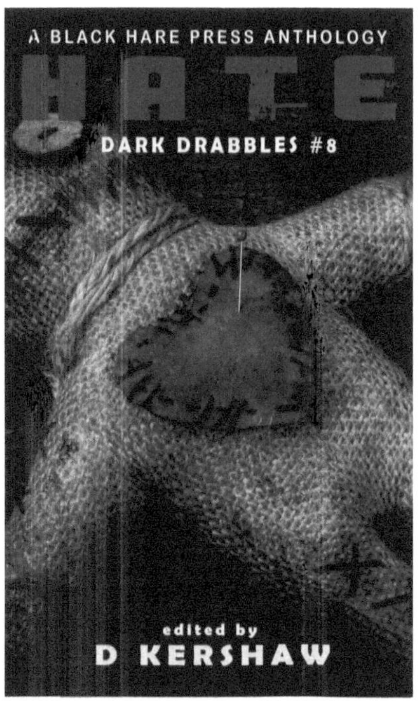

Dark tales of hate and revenge, in bite-sized chunks.

HATE